TRUMPING THE
RACE CARD

TRUMPING THE
RACE CARD

A NATIONAL AGENDA - MOVING
BEYOND RACE AND RACISM

Best Swices for Your Endeavors

RODNEY S. PATTERSON

TRUMPING THE RACE CARD
A NATIONAL AGENDA - MOVING BEYOND RACE AND RACISM

Editors: Lisa Summerour, EdD and Leah Campbell
Cover Design Concept: Ginah Hall
Cover Design: DK Graphics

NCAA Certified Consultant; Stir Fry Productions Certified
Consultant; Global Novations Certified Consultant

iUniverse books may be ordered through booksellers or by contacting:

iUniverse
1663 Liberty Drive
Bloomington, IN 47403
www.iuniverse.com
1-800-Authors (1-800-288-4677)

ISBN: 978-1-4917-7603-2 (sc)
ISBN: 978-1-4917-7604-9 (hc)
ISBN: 978-1-4917-7608-7 (e)

Print information available on the last page.

iUniverse rev. date: 08/28/2015

DEDICATION

I believe I was placed on the planet specifically to help the world deal with racism head on. While I don't claim to possess the stature, status or magnitude of Dr. Martin Luther King Jr., Rosa Parks or Medgar Evers, I do believe that I have a place in the world as an agent of change. I hope my contribution to the dialogue allows our society to view racism from another vantage point, one that encourages us to work together rather than to remain divided.

I first pay tribute to my mother, who raised me to see the good in all people, regardless of their differences. She modeled for me how to love in the presence of hatred and how to look for the humanity in all people. I am eternally grateful for her model.

I dedicate this work to two men who forever changed my life in Burlington, Vermont. Dr. H. Lawrence McCrorey (Larry) served as dean of the College of Allied Heath at the University of Vermont, operating as a one man wrecking crew. He vigilantly attempted to dismantle racism wherever he found it. Larry's voice reverberates in my ears these days as I recall him telling me, "Sometimes, we must remain committed to the cause, even if it means standing alone." As one of just a few blacks in the whitest state in the US, he served as a true drum major for justice.

His lifelong friend, John Tucker, later joined him in Vermont, demonstrating as deep a commitment to abolishing racism as Larry himself. John was both fearless and tenacious in his efforts. Much more outspoken than Larry, John would passionately take on heads of state, institutions, organizations and individuals as if his life depended upon it. John served as director of the Peace and Justice Center of Burlington,

Vermont and through his work; thousands of Vermonters were educated regarding the reality of racism and the need to eradicate the epidemic. Because of Larry and John, I found my passion for the work and my voice in it. I will forever love these men for all that they instilled in me.

I also dedicate this work to the nine individuals who tragically lost their lives while attending bible study at Mother Emmanuel AME Church in Charleston, South Carolina on June 17, 2015. As a pastor who was conducting bible study myself at the time these senseless murders occurred, I felt the impact in a deeply personal way. And as a black person, I found it even more difficult to describe the pain, fear, and sense of volatile vulnerability stemming from such racially motivated hatred. While we can never bring back those who lost their lives that day, I hope and pray my work becomes a significant contribution to that of others who strive to diminish the likelihood of such an occurrence ever happening again.

Finally, I dedicate this work to the individuals who have given their lives to abolishing racism in this country. Much like the lost warriors who fought to gain and maintain our freedom, we are indebted to so many people for their selfless acts of sacrifice. From the abolitionists to the civil rights activists and beyond, to those who fought for racial equality, I pay homage.

TABLE OF CONTENTS

LIST OF FIGURES

FOREWORD BY DR. LEE JUNE, PHD

Trumping the Race Card is a must read and **study** for anyone interested in the areas of diversity, inclusion, and the improvement of race relations. It is unique because Rodney Patterson is someone who is scholarly and has had experience as a practitioner both in the academic and general community. Thus, he presents information that has been tried in or informed by real world experiences.

What I like most about *Trumping the Race Card* is that it blends the scholarly and the practical. It is written in such a way that once the broad issues regarding race are discussed, one is left with concrete and practical things that can be done to improve race relations in this country and the world at large.

Mr. Patterson is well credentialed. He has worked with, been trained by, and /or knows the works of the cutting edge persons in the field. As such, this book draws upon this rich knowledge and experience while breaking new ground. Indeed, we need new ground and tools as we navigate this important field.

In reading *Trumping the Race Card* one will be challenged to think deeply and critically about race and to work toward creating and implementing a new paradigm. The title makes use of a familiar phrase- "the race card" and reframes it for the reader's benefit so that we are empowered to "trump the race card"- the positive, rather than "play the race card- the negative.

Lee N. June, PhD
Professor
Michigan State University

PREFACE

*"...being Latino means being from everywhere and that
is exactly what America is supposed to be about."*
Raquel Cepeda

Trumping the Race Card possesses five parts. We begin by seeking to better understand the meaning of "race card" or "playing the race card." We also explore how playing the race card has become common practice, and how cards are played for nearly every dimension of diversity we can conjure in our minds. Finally, the goal in Chapter 1 is to provide readers with a rationale for addressing the issue in contemporary times, in an effort to prepare for a better future.

In Chapter 2, unpacking the word "racism" is the primary order of business by first returning to the origin and root of the word "race." In elementary school, we were taught that the best way to understand any word was to identify the root word and rediscover the origin of the word. Every word in every language has an origin (i.e. an original meaning) that unveils what was meant when the word was first used or created. To say that the word "racism" is too difficult to define negates the word's origin and root. Once we have examined the origin and root of the word "racism," we discuss the anatomy of the word, as well as its progression and emerging development from other closely associated concepts.

Several questions are addressed during the process of unpacking and clarifying the construction of the concept. Are racism and prejudice the same or are they supporting ideologies? If a person is prejudiced, does that make them racist as well? What makes a person a racist in the true sense of the word?

Uncovering answers to these questions lends enormous support to aiding us in the healing process our nation longs to experience. Once racism is accurately identified and understood, genuine, authentic dialogue ensues, broken relationships mend and empowerment manifests because we are able to point to it, name it, and ultimately work to resolve it. By doing so, we also provide a backdrop against which to frame the idea of trumping the race card.

The third step in the process involves equipping each of us to recognize how racism has, and is currently, manifested within society through systems and institutions. Doing so allows us to fully comprehend how, when and by whom the race card is played and how playing the race card perpetuates racism, as well as our need to hold firmly to the concept of race. So many of us are blinded by the existence of racism and how it operates daily, wreaking havoc in the lives of all people. Each of us is impacted by racism in ways we remain clueless to. Any antibody allowed to enter into the body, unbeknownst and undetected, possesses cascading results and devastating impact. When racism is allowed to run rampant within society due to our inability to identify its presence and mitigating impact, we stand to lose humanity. Consequently, recognizing what ails us has become a human imperative, not just a moral mandate.

After addressing the anatomy and manifestation of racism, we then turn our sights towards solutions. Those invested in uncovering the problem without providing support for creating a solution only exacerbate the problem. People who point to the problem, only to stand back and watch others fix what impacts everyone, often frustrate us. We wish not to be guilty of the same crime and I offer my personal perspective regarding how we might forge ahead as a conglomerate community. Numerous scholars, authors, social activists and concerned citizens alike have offered suggestions and strategies in the past, which have truly enhanced our country and our world. *Trumping the Race Card* is intended to add a voice, energy and effort to the hard work of those courageous souls.

Finally, we end with a summary chapter; bringing closure to all *Trumping the Race Card* was intended to accomplish. I hope that upon finishing this work, you are enlightened, inspired and encouraged to work collaborative towards forming a more perfect union. Therefore, let us forge ahead, beginning with uncovering the origins of the words "race" and "racism," then focusing on the real salient issues at hand, rather than upon the color of our skin.

APPRECIATION

I would like to express my appreciation to the people who contributed most significantly to this work. To the educators who taught me throughout my academic endeavors, beginning with my first teacher, my sister Deborah Wesley. When we were very young, my sister (four years my senior) taught me reading, writing and math before I entered school. Because of her, school came relatively easy for me. Beyond her preliminary instruction, educators in grammar school, high school and college all advanced my learning. Two educators I am compelled to mention specifically, are Dr. Marcus Ahmed and Professor Lou Jeanne Walton. My gratitude and appreciation for each of them is unending.

I also thank Clare Tse, my consulting partner from ProGroup, for pushing me to complete this work and providing editorial support along the journey. I thank Ginah Hall for designing the original cover and DK Graphics for the final cover, models, and marketing material. I thank Latisha Ransom for taking my original manuscript and converting it to book format when I was ready to throw in the towel. She inspired me to press on and provided additional editorial support. Thanks to the Unleaded Group for their input and a special thanks to Leah Campbell for her contribution to the final edit.

Last year, I had the privilege of meeting Dr. Lisa Summerour. She catapulted the project further and faster than my previously mentioned comrades had. Lisa's skilled writing style, coupled with her tenacious project management abilities, brought this work from concept to fruition. From the major editorial overhauling, to the website development, and marketing material preparation, I am forever indebted to her for the significant contribution she made toward the completion of this publication.

Rodney S. Patterson

Most of all, to my wife and life partner, Charlene, who has inspired me throughout the journey to never give up, I owe my life. We spent countless hours dialoguing and rewriting this document for nearly a decade.

Finally, I thank friends and colleagues, Drs. Lee Gartenwartz and Anita Rowe who eagerly contributed their endorsement. I also extend my deepest appreciation and thanks to my greatest mentor, Dr. June Lee, for writing the foreword.

INTRODUCTION

Trumping the Race Card invites you to consider some challenging questions regarding the idiom by examining a few provocative questions. The focus in *Trumping the Race Card* is on addressing the idea of *trumping* the proverbial race card by first examining the origin of race and the impact race has upon society. Even when we attempt to get past our preoccupation with race, something occurs that catapults us back into the time warp of yesteryear, when race mattered more than any other aspect of a person's identity. Perhaps in our efforts to return to the origin of the word "race," we can identify a remedy for what separates us. If there is any real chance of us trumping the race card, deconstructing the enormous race-based skyscrapers we have constructed in nearly every system and institution operating within society must occur.

Our greatest opportunity for success lies within our willingness to confront the issues of race and racism head on. Rather than treating the conversation as off limits, taboo or too difficult to discuss, the need for fresh, authentic information-based dialogue will allow us to face our fears and work towards solutions. One of our major challenges has been our inability to agree upon common language that seeks to inform rather than blame and shame. This often causes a segment of the population to wallow in guilt for the sins of their ancestors.

A significant goal of this work has been to examine the issues of race and racism by removing the emotional baggage associated with the terms while focusing upon the parts we all contribute to; perpetuation and resolution. We seek to identify the origins of both terms, the manifestation that results when they are in play and the impact they have upon our everyday lives.

Rodney S. Patterson

W.E.B. DuBois once suggested that the greatest problem of the 21st century would be overcoming the impact of race and racism. Now is the best time to attempt to do so. We are the generation left with the daunting task so that future generations are not plagued by, or left with, the same problems our ancestors faced. What we do will determine the place race occupies in the lives of our descendants.

CHAPTER 1

*"We have made enormous progress in teaching everyone
that racism is bad. Where we seem to have dropped the
ball… is in teaching people what racism actually is."*
Jon Stewart

MOVING BEYOND RACE
AND RACISM

One of the most politically charged and emotionally loaded phrases of
the present century is the terminology "playing the race card." Regardless
of how one frames or contextualizes the idiom, it is hardly positive; in
fact, it's wholly derogatory. Yet, the phrase is used so frequently by so
many powerful, highly visible individuals, people seldom flinch when
they hear it, unless it's used in reference to someone from their own
"race." Given the history associated with the words "race" and "racism"
in the United States, who among us wishes to be accused of playing
the race card?

A segment of our society was raised to believe that race cards
were reserved for those identified as disadvantaged, marginalized or
disenfranchised in society; you know, *minorities*. In reality, race can
never be used as an advantage to one group without simultaneously
being a disadvantage to another.[1, 2]

I interpret the work of authors Peggy McIntosh, an American
feminist and anti-racism activist, and Frances Kendall, an academic
and expert in the fields of multicultural education and the concept of

1

white privilege, as suggesting that every person, regardless of race, has been awarded the proverbial race card to play at their own convenience. Yet race card statements remind us of our differences, and the impact of those differences, in human interactions. They serve as a reminder that we are in need of authentic, constructive dialogue that will help us achieve a shared collective conscience powerful enough to trump racial disparity.

Growing up playing cards in Chicago, I quickly learned that the primary function of a trump card was to nullify the impact of all other cards in the deck. Lay down a trump card in a game of bid whist, for instance, and the highest card in any particular suit is rendered powerless. If we, as a society, learn to trump the race card, race will no longer have the power to influence. The goal of trumping the race card is to diminish and eventually eradicate the power that race has wielded for centuries, both within the United States and around the globe.

Each of us possesses more than just one card specific to our individual identities. We hold our own deck of cards, which is comprised of a complex compilation of interconnected diversity components, identified in Gartenwartz and Rowe's "Dimensions of Diversity" wheel, illustrated in Figure 1.[3.]

At times, when we have been treated in a disparaging manner, we seek to identify the cause and wonder whether or not the treatment resulted from a perceived difference we possessed. In the absence of information, many of us revert to a subconscious examination of our own dimensions of diversity components. Was I treated that way because of my race? Was it my gender? My sexual orientation? My religious beliefs? My level or tenure in the organization? Is it that I'm short, tall, fat, or thin? Is it my age? What is it about me?

It is obvious that some of the components on the dimensions of diversity wheel are apparent immediately. In many instances, it's easy to distinguish between old and young, male and female.

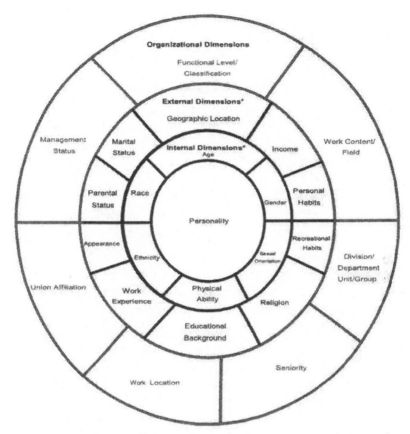

Figure 1 Diverse Teams at Work, Gardenswartz & Rowe | Internal Dimensions and External adapted from Marilyn Loden and Julie Rosener, Workforce America; Business One Irwin, 1991

In some instances, race too is evident from the outside. While it is true that bias and prejudice concerning age and sex create heated debates, conversations about race remain some of the most arduous conversations on the list. From birth to death, race is a differentiator over which we have no control. And during our lives we routinely talk about, and face-off over, race. Invariably, I have to believe that we want to make a positive difference in how race is perceived and how it affects our community.

Racially charged dialogues aren't new. America's Civil War (1861 – 1865) was based on the fractious issue of slavery. Nine decades later, in the 1954 case of *Brown v. Board of Education*, race was the basis for the US Supreme Court's ruling that segregated schools were

3

unconstitutional. This was followed by another seminal moment in the civil rights movement when, in 1955 in Montgomery, Alabama, black citizens protested against racial discrimination in the city's bus service.

The 1992 Los Angeles riots raged for six days, creating a chasm between races. The tension that boiled under this city's surface reverberated through theaters in 2004, when the film "Crash" took home three Academy Awards. Inspired by a real-life carjacking incident on L.A.'s Wilshire Boulevard, producer/director Paul Haggis dared to expose racism in an era that had supposedly gotten past all that.

Racism was at the epicenter of the 2008 presidential election. For the first time in the history of the United States, an African American was the top candidate for the Democratic Party. Barack Obama won the 2008 presidential election decisively, garnering 69,297,997 popular and 365 electoral votes, compared to John McCain's respective totals of 59,597,520 and 173.[4] The preoccupation with race only seemed to increase in 2012, when President Obama won his second term with 65,446,032 popular and 332 electoral votes, compared to Mitt Romney's respective totals of 60,589,084 and 206.[5]

Other headline-grabbing incidents that fueled the debate over race and equality in recent years included comments made from the pulpit of President Obama's former church home, Trinity United Church of Christ in Chicago, IL. Outspoken former pastor, Dr. Jeremiah Wright, received harsh criticism and sparked more racial debates with a sermon that blamed the United States for the attacks that took place on September 11, 2001. Ward Connelly's work to dismantle affirmative action in California tops the list. The University of Michigan deserves an honorable mention for its landmark case amending the state's constitution in 2006 and restructuring the political process to put members of racially diverse groups at a disadvantage regarding admissions policies. Any time an issue such as Michigan's rises to the level of the Supreme Court, the media and citizenry alike become polarized. Fingers are pointed, accusations are lobbed, and our country is reset to zero, back to pre-civil rights times.

The tragic deaths of Trayvon Martin, in Florida, Michael Brown in Ferguson, Missouri, and Eric Garner in New York serve as prime examples of how race continues to be viewed as a motivator of despicable acts, as well as an influence in how we interpret certain events. The racially charged opinion of Clive Bundy, whose recorded comments appeared in a New York Times article on April 24, 2014, served as an in-your-face reminder that racism still divides people.[6] Yet, the "chink in the armor"[7] comment lobbed by ESPN's editor, Anthony Federico, at New York Knicks player, Jeremy Lin, begs us to evaluate the question of racism.

Let us not forget recent events like the dispute involving young teens attending a mixed-race pool party in McKinney, Texas, or the tragic massacre at Mother Emmanuel AME Church in Charleston, South Carolina. These two incidents, along with many others, caused me to wonder; do we have a concise and accurate understanding of what racism really is? Many people lump each of these situations into the same category as incidents of extreme racism. But are they?

Is it possible for us to talk about racism when we seem to have multiple and conflicting definitions, or no real working definition at all, on which we can agree? We often hear pundits, politicians, the general public and even academicians opine about incidents they deem racist. For instance, Giuliana Rancic of *E! Fashion Police* commented on actress Zendaya Coleman's hair by saying, "I feel like she smells like patchouli oil ... or maybe weed."[8] Was that comment in bad taste, or was it a racist statement?

The chances of resolving an issue that has plagued us for nearly six centuries remain elusive until we can agree on an accurate and adequate definition of racism. We need clarity; otherwise, we are attempting to treat symptoms without clearly diagnosing the problem.

On numerous occasions, I have found myself wishing I could sit across the table from political scientists and pundits Rush Limbaugh, Sean Hannity, Glen Beck, Rachel Maddow, Condoleezza Rice, or my favorite satirist, Bill Maher. I imagine asking each of them, "How do you define racism? How do you determine who, or what, is, or is not, racist?" I wonder how much their answers would shift if they operated with a single, agreed-upon definition of racism that was based on anthropological and sociological research. It boils down to two critical questions:

1. What are the benefits of identifying an accurate definition of racism?
2. What are the dangers associated with inaccurately defining racism?

In countless workshops I have conducted nationwide, participants from all walks of life responded to my question, "What would the benefit be of identifying an accurate definition of racism?" Uniformly, they concluded that having an accurate definition of racism would provide the best opportunity to address the issue. In other words, when we understand what racism really is, we can teach others about it and work to abolish it. Or at least, we can work to diminish the negative impact left in its wake. Conversely, by failing to accurately define racism, we render ourselves incapable of resolving any issues related to its impact.

When I was young, my grandmother would say to me, "Son, you can't fix what you don't understand." When entering into battle, the first thing you need to understand is who the enemy is. Otherwise, you could do harm to individuals who might be allies and supporters. The same holds true concerning racism. The innocent suffer accidental calamity due to us mistakenly identifying them as the enemy.

In our battle against racism in the United States, friendly fire has created as many casualties as enemy attacks. In addition, in some instances, well-intended individuals have engaged in hurtful and harmful acts because they were unaware of the impact of their behavior. Labeling someone as a racist may be an emotional reaction to nearly any racially charged situation. Because of our wide range of perspectives, we can wound one another with word choices, whether we intend to or not.

Contemporary authors and opinion-makers such as Paul Kivel, Frances Kendall, Joe Feagin and Derald Wing Sue have undertaken the arduous task of clarifying racism as a term without casting blame, shame and guilt among white and Caucasian individuals. Seeking to blame, shame or create guilt immobilizes people. Whites and other racially diverse people must assume dual responsibility for the perpetuation of racism in our world. However, I make the distinction between dual responsibility and mutual responsibility. Mutual responsibility assumes that the responsibility is equally shared between the two parties. Dual responsibility recognizes and acknowledges that both parties play a role, but not necessarily an equal role. Still, the roles remain distinctly essential. While all races share mutual responsibility for perpetuating racism, the degrees to which they are responsible can differ drastically. I speak more about these differences in later chapters.

Racism will remain a problem until we resolve the root cause as a community. Until we get to that pivotal point in time that we share a common, research-based definition of racism, racism's negative impact will continue to affect us into our future. We, as a people, will revert to old patterns and nothing will change. My earnest desire is to offer a salient solution that prevents this from becoming the case for future generations.

From an anthropological, biological, and sociological perspective, we need to identify and celebrate the universal similarities among us. In essence, we need to embrace our oneness. The goal of any relevant conversation going forward should be to establish a specific and universal definition of racism that transcends skin color. From the 30,000-foot perspective, we can see what others have overlooked because they were too deep into the fray. Once we have identified and acknowledged our similarities, we can remove barriers to the conversation and reexamine racism's impact upon society, especially within workplace.

I am not suggesting that we remove emotion from the dialogue. By its very nature race often incites and ignites an emotional discussion. The value in retaining the emotion in the dialogue is that emotion fuels change. Candor can spur new thought, establish essential understanding and solidify unity. That is the oneness we seek, the condition of humankind that can surpass the limitations of racism.

CHAPTER 2

"In order to get beyond race, we must first take account of race."
Harry Blackmun, US Supreme Court Justice

FROM RACISM TO DIVERSITY AND BEYOND RACE TO CULTURE

I often share with people how my journey into the world of diversity training began. It started while growing up as young black kid on the south side of Chicago. In a city Martin Luther King Jr. once characterized as one of the most segregated cities in the North, I lived the realities of racism close-up and personal as a very young child.

Very few people are afforded the luxury of having a single thread woven through their personal and professional experiences, resulting in a perfect tapestry as I have experienced in my life. My close encounters ranged from fleeing irate white males who chased me and a group of black friends from the predominantly white populated area of Bridgeport, to being on my high school fan bus and getting pelted with rocks and bottles while attending a basketball game in the Marquette Park area of Chicago. Those experiences taught me that I was different because I was black and that made me unwelcomed.

I would leave Chicago to attend college at Valparaiso University, where it was immediately obvious that I was not like most students on campus. My skin color, hair texture, facial features and cultural experiences were not common amongst my classmates. Again, I experienced that feeling of being unwelcomed by a significant segment of the population. A close encounter with local KKK members nearly caused my dad to force my return home from college for good. I am very appreciative that he allowed me to remain and face fears. Doing so gave me one of my first opportunities to develop positive relationships after overcoming a racially charged negative experience. Subsequently, I established what have become life-long relationships with mentors, friends, and great acquaintances, many of whom happen to be white. My ability to develop strong, successful cross-racial friendships became critical life lessons to which I attribute many of my future successes. They honed my ability to overcome racial barriers initially intended to intimidate me.

By the time I arrived at Michigan State University (MSU) to begin graduate school, I had learned to feel very comfortable within a predominantly white institution. I established a support system comprised of a multi-racial network of friends, mentors and allies. Because my mentors and social network were so diverse at Valparaiso University, I entered graduate school well prepared for a similar experience. During that time, I learned about racial theories, advancing my early underpinnings about racism from my undergraduate social work class. It was at MSU that I was selected to conduct my first staff development training session on diversity.

Diversity at the time was the new buzzword designed to advance the national dialogue beyond race and racial sensitivity. But the real growth opportunity occurred when I graduated from MSU and became director of multicultural affairs at the University of Vermont. University of Vermont president, Lattie Coor, had just published his plan for establishing greater racial diversity on campus through student and faculty recruitment efforts, scholarships, and broader curriculum offerings. The university implemented a Race and Culture course required for nearly every entering freshman in 1988. As a new hire, I was asked to teach the course, which led to my participation in a faculty colloquium conducted by Dr. Phil Royster. Dr. Royster introduced me to the pejorative nature associated with the concept of race.

Once classes began, I quickly ascertained how teaching about race and culture differed drastically from any of my former teaching experiences. While students came eager to engage, they found the

9

subject of race difficult to discuss. Many students resented feeling forced to take a course loaded with such volatility. It required a vulnerability most were unwilling to embrace. My greatest discovery involved altering my pedagogical approach once I realized that I could never experience true success by jamming concepts down the throats of students and referring to it as learning.

Whenever concepts are forced upon students, they regurgitate them, as they might any other foreign material introduced into their systems. Rather than sharing facts, figures, dates, and data, I transitioned to the Socratic approach of asking the right questions, in the right manner, hoping students would experience personal epiphanies. Focusing upon culture first, rather than race, created a *safer* environment that was more conducive to fostering constructive and authentic dialogue.

Culture and Diversity

The mid-80s ushered in the era of diversity, shifting the focus from debates about race and gender differences to dialogues about other aspects of difference; namely, a broader range of cultural differences. White people in general, white males in particular, grew weary of continuously being identified as "the problem" within society. Workshops focused upon racial sensitivity and gender inequity were somewhat effective, yet still divisive. This meant that some individuals experienced personal insights, while others left seminars disgusted and frustrated, vowing never to return to another one of *those* sessions. Workshop facilitators aiming to invite people from all walks of life to the dialogue table introduced the focus on diversity, and in some instances it was effective.

I was living in Vermont, which was referred to as the "whitest state in the country" as recently as April of 2014, sharing the title of least diverse part of the country with Maine.[1] As a new professional, I was repeatedly requested to conduct diversity workshops. I vividly recall preparing for one of my initial sessions at the University of Vermont.

While driving to the session, I had an idea. I drove to the local supermarket and purchased several different types of apples, oranges, bananas, melons, grapes, peaches, and pears. I incorporated these fruits into my presentation to provide a visual aid. First, I used the apples to discuss how different varieties of the same fruit reflected diversity. For example, some apples were best used for baking pies, while other apples were better for making a fruit salad. My analogy then extended to how one could have a greater appreciation for consuming fruit salad, rather than settling for a single apple. Yet, each fruit maintained its own distinct flavor and texture while combined in the same container.

As time passed, I began to hear my fruit and fruit salad analogies being shared in other workshops. If imitation is the greatest form of flattery, suffice it to say, I was beyond flattered to have proof that my fruit-filled presentation made having difficult discussions about race and cultural diversity easier for workshop participants and the facilitators responsible for encouraging that dialogue. Thus began my steadied career as a diversity educator, focused upon shifting workshop participants away from more intense conversations about race to more palatable dialogue about cultural diversity.

Inevitably, race remained on the radar as an unavoidable and divisively toxic topic. The beating of Rodney King, by Los Angeles police officers who were later acquitted, brought the issue of race immediately back to a place of volatile, media frenzied prominence; proving that society was still not ready to address the issue of race, absence polarization. I watched the same dynamic manifest at the University of Vermont's campus once the verdict was announced and realized we could not avoid the conversation.

Shortly thereafter, MSU rehired me as assistant to the vice president of student affairs for multicultural development. I spent my fifteen years there refining my knowledge, skills, and delivery as a diversity practitioner. Hired by ProGroup, a consulting company based in Minneapolis, Minnesota, I offered diversity workshops to a plethora of Fortune 500 and 100 companies; I learned how to artfully invite people to explore their own biases, prejudices, and assumptions in a disarming manner. I witnessed participants leave workshops ranting and raving about having made fresh discoveries regarding their own biases, prejudices and assumptions. Finally, I felt like I was uncovering a way to invite people to the table to discuss issues concerning diversity and race, without feeling threatened, guilty or shamed to the point of immobilization and disengagement. I discovered what I referred to as an emotional/psychological anesthetic that made folks comfortable enough to have deep, authentic and impassioned discussions about extremely sensitive topics.

My experiences at (MSU) and ProGroup exposed me to even greater diversity education gurus. I was privileged for the opportunity to work directly with individuals like Lee Mun Wah, Paul Kivel, Francis Kendall and other giants in the field. I maintained a working affiliation with ProGroup, which was later acquired by Novations before it merged with Global Lead. ProGroup, Novations and Global Lead once independently represented the three largest, and arguably the most cutting edge, firms offering diversity education. I obtained both theory and practice from the "best-of-the-best," positioning me to gain exposure to some of the most relevant information in the market. Still, diversity education was in no way viewed as the cure-all antidote for what plagued society. While diversity proved easier to discuss than racism, people either viewed diversity as a code word for racism and sexism or considered it a smoke screen, designed to lure them into blame-laden discussions about those deeper, more taboo issues.

After two decades of focusing upon diversity, many organizations complained about suffering from what Trevor Wilson referred to in his work as "diversity fatigue." He described diversity fatigue as the overwhelming frustration organizations and diversity practitioners experienced that resulted in minor returns on employee engagement, productivity and the company's bottom line.[2] The focus on diversity took us beyond the fixation on race, but we apparently still have a ways to go.

From Diversity to Human Equity

Wilson, an author, consultant, and leader in the field of diversity, recently introduced to the lexicon a provocative concept he refers to as "human equity."[3] Although working primarily in Canada and other international locales, Wilson's work is pregnant with global possibilities. Before I gained exposure to Wilson's work, I shifted, paradigmatically, from emphasizing diversity and inclusion to highlighting engagement as the key success factor. Diversity centered on differences; inclusion involved appreciating and embracing those differences. Engagement was the missing element in the evolutionary process.

Engagement was not a new concept. In the 1990's the term "student engagement" became prevalent within higher education. Theorists like Alexander Astin and George Kuh researched the relationship between student engagement and retention, concluding that the more engaged students were, the more successfully they matriculated through to academy.[4, 5]

Almost simultaneously, corporations began measuring employee and customer engagement. Gallup's research highlights the correlation between employee engagement and profitability. According to Gallup, the higher the employee engagement index, the higher the profits. Engaged employees consistently tender discretionary effort on the job.[6] Consequently, I adopted a mantra during workshops: "When companies get engagement right, diversity will often take care of itself."

My simple message was when companies focus upon making certain every employee is fully engaged at work, regardless of their dimension of diversity, they will put forth discretionary effort. Highly engaged employees serve as the company's best public relations team, attracting more talent and more customers. And when diverse employees become highly engaged, they attract other diverse employees as well.

Once my attention shifted towards engagement, I sought a strategy for significantly advancing engagement within organizations. Wilson's work provided the missing link to positively advance the needle on employee and customer engagement. In Wilson's book, *The Human Equity Advantage*, he defined human capital as the knowledge, skills and intangible assets employees brought to work everyday. He found that most managers lacked proficiency uncovering the requisite knowledge and skills their direct reports possessed, and worse yet, completely overlooked the employees' intangible skills. As a result, the knowledge skills and assets of the employee were under-utilized, leading to lower levels of productivity, thus engagement. Human equity can only surface by optimizing the human capital of an employee, i.e. the knowledge, skills and intangibles assets, through the lens of diversity. Rather than ignoring the differences an individual possesses, we learn to fully utilize and maximize the differences reflected in their full range of knowledge, skills and intangible assets.[7]

I was most intrigued by Wilson's use of the word "equity" rather than "equality." The word "equality" emulates from civil rights and women's suffrage vernacular. Unfortunately, some people become tense and withdraw as soon as the word is used. To clarify the distinction between equity and equality, I often ask workshop participants, "Who in the room has more than one child or was raised in a family with at least one other sibling?" Usually, most respond affirmatively. I then ask if their parents (or if they, as parents) treat their children exactly the same, i.e. equally. In most instances participants admit they don't treat their children the same, nor were they treated the same as their siblings. When asked why not, their response has consistently been, "Because we were different." As a follow up question, I ask, "Is it possible to treat people differently while still maintaining a level of fairness?" The response is always positive.

Equal treatment requires us to treat everyone exactly the same. Equity or equitable treatment requires that we recognize the differences and nuances, and still treat people appropriately, while insuring we maintain the highest level of fairness. Equity focuses upon fairness and equality focuses on sameness. Therefore, human equity is about maximizing the knowledge, skills and intangible assets of people while demonstrating fairness.[8]

Through human equity, I found a concept that resonated with all people from all walks of life, at all levels within an organization. I believe people want to experience their highest level of engagement, at work, in school, in social organizations, churches, synagogues or wherever they may reside. I believe they want to be recognized, optimized, and fully utilized as part of creating positive outcomes. Like the dialogue on diversity was intended to do, human equity invites people to the table. However, the human equity dialogue has proven to be a much more digestible meal. Even those who suffer from "diversity fatigue" tend to gravitate to the idea of human equity, perceiving real possibilities for positive change.

When human equity is viewed as the ultimate goal, we begin the dialogue from a position of unity and strength. As a result, all energies and efforts are directed at establishing an equitable environment. I argue in this work how racism challenges our ability to create a truly equitable environment. Whenever and wherever racism is present, human equity is threatened. The two ideas can never simultaneously coexist. Thusly, I no longer suggest for companies or communities to begin by attempting to tackle racism within their respective environments. Instead, I encourage them to first seek to develop an environment where human equity truly exists. By beginning with the end in mind, we can address what prevents us from reaching our desired state.

CHAPTER 3

"I realize that definitions spark controversy and disagreement, but I'm ok with that. I'd rather we debate the meaning of words that are important to us than not discuss them at all. We need common language to help us create awareness and understanding..." Brene' Brown

THE ROOT AND ORIGIN OF RACISM

Ask ten people to define racism, and it is likely you would end up with ten different definitions. I would wager you would get the same results if you asked leading media personalities, pundits, and political leaders about their definitions of racism. I had an occasion to do just that, after being accused of engaging in a racist act by a Burlington, Vermont newspaper reporter. I simply asked the reporter to define racism. Not surprisingly, the reporter proved incapable of providing an accurate definition. Too often, people label others as racist when they cannot even provide a clear definition of the term "racism" themselves.

So what makes racism so difficult to define? How does one converse about something they don't understand? Therein lies the problem. Too often, we render opinions and generalizations about critical matters without an understanding of the topic at hand. In elementary school, we were taught to look first at the root of the word to establish its meaning. We were then advised to research the origin of the word. But the word racism contains both a root and an origin seldom researched and often overlooked.

When people are asked to define racism, most respond by saying it is prejudiced views about people based upon their race. The *Oxford English*

Dictionary defines racism as, "A belief or ideology that all members of each racial group possess characteristics or abilities specific to that race, especially to distinguish it as being either superior or inferior to another racial group."[1] *Merriam-Webster* defines racism as, "A belief that race is the primary determinant of human traits and capabilities, and racial differences produce an inherent superiority of a particular racial group, and that it is also the prejudices based on such a belief."[2] Finally, the *Macquarie Dictionary*, the authoritative source of English usage in Australia, defines racism as, "The belief that human races have distinctive characteristics which determine their respective cultures, usually involving the idea that one's own race is superior and has a right to rule or dominate others."[3]

Although prejudiced views and opinions are a component of racism, such oversimplified definitions fall short of rendering a thorough understanding of a very complex concept. Debates suggest that racism has many definitions and multiple meanings, making the term quite confusing to grasp. While true on one level, the word "racism" has a simple definition as well. I contend the word itself is no different than any other word in the English language and therefore, like any word, can be easily defined.

When attempting to accurately define racism, we must first identify the root of the word and return to its origin. The root of the word racism is, of course, race. To fully comprehend the root word "race," we turn to science for insight. By grounding our efforts in a scholarly review, we further lend support to effectively trumping the race card.

The Science of Race

Two schools of scientific thought provide critical enlightenment regarding the concept of race. Anthropologists and biologists are experts in the field of science relative to understanding the realities and complexities of race. In fact, if someone wishes to discuss the issue of race, yet fails to provide scientific support, their argument lacks validity. Dr. Audrey Smedley writes in her book, *Race in North America,* that anthropologists are essentially responsible for conducting research about mankind and the races of mankind, so these areas of concentration lay at the heart of anthropology. Furthermore, since the mid to late 1800s, there has been a progressive elimination of the word and concept of race from anthropological textbooks. For at least the past two centuries, anthropologists have argued there is no such thing as race and that race only serves as a myth or an abstraction. Smedley further asserts that biologists concur with anthropologists in that biologists find no scientific support for the retention of the term or concept of race.[4]

Dr. Dave Unander, a geneticist, writes in *Shattering the Myth of Race* that race is a myth. Prior to the year 1400, the word "race" as we currently use it did not exist. Still, Muslim Arab slave traders developed a theory of African inferiority based on their religious beliefs. Dr. Unander debunks the realistic possibility of race, because each one of us evolved from "one combination out of a minimum of some eight million times eight million possibilities."[5] This means that our ability to compartmentalize race into some neat, simple package is really absurd, thereby suggesting race has no scientific foundation.

As far back as 1758, in the tenth edition of *Systemae Naturae*, Carolus Linnaeus' work helped characterize the concept of race when he made a distinction between the world's continental population and proposed four subcategories of Homo sapiens: Americanus, Asiaticus, Africanus, and Europeanus.[6] In 1795, Johann Friedrich Blumenbach expanded on this concept when he used physical and racial distinctions to categorize the human species into five varieties: Caucasian, Mongolian, Ethiopian, American, and Malay.[7] In the video series *Race: The Power of Illusion: The Differences Between Us*, produced by Larry Adelman, race is exhaustively discussed and the conclusion remains the same: race as we know it and use it has no scientific foundation.[8] The work of The Canadian Broadcasting Company in the video *Skin Deep: The Science of Race* reiterates the same message. [9] A research project originally created in Geneva, Switzerland entitled *All of Us Are Related, Each of Us is Unique* was translated to English by Professor Marshall Segall and produced by Syracuse University. It draws the same conclusion; race simply does not exist.[10]

If leading contemporary scientists have repeatedly asserted that race does not exist, the claim that there is only one race, the human race, is also inaccurate. If there is no such thing as race, we are not part of a human race; we are simply human beings or Homo sapiens.

Consequently, Jimmy the Greek's on air comment in January 1988, when he stated that blacks were athletically superior based upon their racial identity, was dead wrong.[11] Blacks are neither athletically superior nor inferior solely because of their race. Nor are people of European or Asian decent academically or intellectually superior because of their race. The important message then to share with students, at all academic levels, from all walks of life, is that intelligence is not related to skin color.

Herrnstein and Murray's controversial book, *The Bell Curve,* purports that intelligence is one of the, if not the, most important factors correlated with economic, social, and professional success in the United States. Moreover, the authors maintain that the importance of race is increasing. While that may be true, they base many of their conclusions regarding intellectual success on standard IQ testing, which has proven to be a less-than-perfect way of measuring intelligence across a diverse population of varied circumstances. Many people argue that IQ tests are riddled with cultural biases and present a false picture of native intellectual differences among ethnic, cultural and social groups. While blacks as a whole may score lower than Caucasians on standard IQ tests, and Caucasians score lower than Asians, those differences may be more indicative of flaws in the psychometrics than actual differences in native intelligence among racial classifications. So when Herrnstein and Murray argue that United States immigration policies should favor one group of people over another, they perpetuate racial stereotypes and discrimination.[12]

While scientists increasingly debunk historically constructed myths of inherent racial superiority, many generations of children have suffered from the belief that intellectual superiority is racially driven. Jane Elliot uncovered the damaging impact of promoting racial inferiority in her film, *A Class Divided.*

Her third grade class of all white students in Riceville, Iowa was divided into two distinct groups based upon their eye color. When tasked with reading through a card stack and timed for their level of efficiency, proficiency and accuracy, she found the children who wore collars depicting their assigned inferiority status performed far worse than their pre-research performance. When their collars were removed, their proficiency scores were higher than their pre-research performance.[13]

When people are taught race can never predetermine performance, we can decrease academic performance disparities currently existing between ethnically diverse communities. Only when people are taught that race should never be used to influence or impact performance will we make progress in diminishing disparities that exist within ethnically diverse communities and academia. However, as long as children view themselves as academically inferior because of race or ethnicity, closing the gaps between whites and racially diverse people will remain elusive.

The Social Construction of Race

If race does not exist from a scientific perspective, how can race, or for that matter, racism, exist? And why do we even use the term "race?"

According to the work of sociologists and other social scientists, race was constructed based upon the pre-existing social manifestations and ramifications associated with it. Smedley insists that the concept is culturally manufactured, coinciding with the dawn of European expansion. Race neither was, nor ever has been, a proven, scientific reality, yet race does operate as a social reality originating in the languages of the French, German, Dutch, Portuguese, English, Irish and Italian, to name just a few.[14]

Smedley maintains there is a distinction between the concept of race and ethnicity. Although often used synonymously, the terms carry distinct meanings. Race is typically associated with biological, phenotypic, physical characteristics serving as measures of demarcation in human variation. Ethnicity, on the other hand, relates to one's culture rather than one's race. Culture is defined as a common set of beliefs, customs, practices, values and languages shared by a group of people, yet culture is not bound by time or space. Groups of people share cultural aspects regardless of where they are located, the time span of their existence or any physical differences they possess.[15]

Ethnicity is related to culture, not race. In fact, each ethnic group contains several racially categorized groups. For example, within the "white race" are:

- Europeans
- Germans
- Italians
- French
- Dutch
- Scandinavians

Those ethnic groups identified within the "Asian race" include:

- Chinese
- Japanese
- Filipinos
- Hmong
- Vietnamese
- Pacific Islanders

Individuals who identify as "African" or "North American Indian" are referred to as tribes rather than ethnic groups. Even the group identified as "Hispanic/Latino," (which is a US census-contrived categorization, not a distinct racial group) is used to represent several different ethnic groups, including Mexican, Puerto Rican, Dominican, Cuban, Venezuelan and others.

People of Middle Eastern heritage are often categorized as both white and Asian. In his book entitled *Whitewash*, John Tehranian, a law professor at Chapman University, mentioned the confusion associated with Middle Easterners walking in both worlds. Much like Smedley, Tehranian exposes the lack of scientific underpinnings for the retention of race as a basis for classifying people. However, Tehranian paints a detailed picture of the social and legal construction of race.[16] The number of so-called racial groups, or what should more appropriately be deemed "ethnic groups," expands exponentially on a frequent basis according to the most recent United States census information.

The bottom line is this; although distinct and inaccurate as a scientifically proven identifier, "race" continues to matter, especially to those who keep count of the number of people from different groups.

Race Matters

In our country, census data counts, particularly because demographic data collection, reporting, and criminal records provide daily reminders to us of the divisions between humankind. We are a society preoccupied with numbers. Tracking the number of people of color in the workforce, on a college campus, in the penal system, receiving housing loans, dying from chronic diseases, or involved in the last election clearly informs us that for many people, race still matters.

Media headlines were saturated with reports about who voted for Governor Romney or President Obama along racial lines in 2012. Court systems are filled with cases alleging racial discrimination in the workplace. Local and regional municipalities and university campus police departments have a plethora of race-related hate crime incident reports crossing their desks daily.

When the opportunity arises, countless numbers of blacks, Latinos, Asians, and native indigenous people share stories about dealing with everyday racism. Even white people share experiences of racial incidents. No question about it, race does exist as a concept, and racism is alive and well in the United States, despite the absence of scientifically validated biological and anthropological evidence. Our collective experiences confirm its existence, because we have socially constructed the concept.

What would then precipitate the need to concoct an idea lacking a scientific foundation? And, if the measures we have used to differentiate people on the basis of race have no true merit, why still use them? Why do we constantly and continually refer to people in ways that have no real meaning or true utility? Why do we continue to use racial classifications, if there is no scientific support for doing so?

Does using racial classifications cause us to perpetuate the use of our so-called race card?

Why Race Was Needed

The idea of differentiating or categorizing people is not new. We have classified people throughout history, with the most notable classification system being the demographic tracking of the United States Census Bureau, which started tracking US citizens in 1790.[17] The Census Bureau reports that it uses race classifications for:

- The benefit of Federal programs to make policy decisions
- Legislative redistricting
- To promote equal employment opportunities
- To assess racial disparities.[18]

We have categorized people on employment and college applications, and in affirmative action reports, for decades. We learn to differentiate at very early stages of our human development. Even during biblical times, people from different tribes and geographic locations were distinguished. Yet, the idea of distinguishing people based strictly upon race, as Smedley mentioned earlier, emerged as an expansionist paradigm during the 16th century.[19] However, European expansionists did not create racial distinctions solely due to their disdain for dark-skinned people. A survey of US history informs us that indentured servitude pre-empted the practice of using enslaved Africans as a labor source in the New World.

Historians document the first indentured servants as arriving in the New World in 1607, while the first Africans arrived in 1619. Ironically, as no official laws for slavery existed at the time, these first African immigrants were basically treated with the same rights, and given the same entitlements, as the indentured servants from England who had arrived before them. As indentured servants, immigrants could earn their freedom by working for periods often contracted to last from four to seven years. Some contracts even guaranteed a minimum of 25 acres of land, corn, cows, clothing and arms.[20]

Unfortunately, nearly 40 percent of the indentured servants who emigrated from England died before their seven-year terms were completed.[21] This, coupled with landowners feeling threatened by freed servants demanding their own land,[22] left many looking for other options. It didn't help that run away indentured servants who were white had a better chance of assimilating into the population. Whether it was because of some of these issues, or a coincidence that satisfied landowner dilemmas, slavery laws were instituted in Massachusetts in 1641 and in Virginia in 1661. The minimal freedoms blacks had were gone, as landowners shifted to the more renewable and less expensive labor force of enslaved Africans and blacks.[23]

Enslaved Africans survived unspeakable inhumanities while being transported across the African continent to be loaded as cargo onto slave ships, only to endure even more horrible conditions while being transported along the middle passage. As the population of enslaved Africans increased, so did extreme forms of racial bias and discrimination within the United States. Thusly, expansionists and their supporters concocted justifications for their dehumanizing actions using mythical, arbitrary and fictitious scientific underpinnings.

Slavery, at its inception, was far less about race and racism and more about economic expansion, power and privilege. In fact, Smedley reminds us that classism gave birth to racism, creating a need to differentiate, and worse yet, discriminate.[24]

In the film *Race: The Power of An Illusion*, the filmmaker reminds us of Thomas Jefferson's direct authorship in the *Declaration of Independence* "that all men are created equal."[25] But, in his *Notes on the State of Virginia*, Jefferson characterized black men as inferior in the endowments of both body and mind and so they were justifiably not afforded the same rights and privileges as whites.[26] What began as an economically driven condition, quickly emerged as impassioned, heart-felt repulsion.

Differentiating Not Discriminating

Categorizing people based upon factious racial differences alone is moderately damaging. The problems associated with racism have never been based upon differentiating or distinguishing one group of people from another. The real problem has been about discriminating against those whom we differentiate. Differentiating people based upon language, dress, customs, core values, beliefs, and rituals is common practice. However, our problem as a society stems from how we view those we distinguish as different from ourselves. When differentiation leads to disparate treatment, significantly greater issues can result. Many forms of slavery existed long before the development of racial taxonomy and race classification. History teaches us how slavery, and ways of differentiating people, were not based upon race until fairly recently.

Surprisingly, Dr. Unander reported that biblical slavery was not based upon racial differences and racism. The word "race," as used in contemporary times, was a post-dated concept. Consequently, race-based slavery was neither an issue nor a factor.[27] The Bible did not directly, nor specifically, mention race as it is referenced in this book; hence, the bible makes no direct reference to racism. Once race became the grounds for categorizing and differentiating people from one another, the stage was set for the creation of a racist ideology and the construction of a racist society.

The Anatomy of an Ism

The progression from a simple bias to the development of an ism is illustrated in figure 2. I first learned of the theory behind the progression from a bias to an ism while attending the Texas A&M University Summer Institute on Diversity in 2000. Dr. Becky Pettit, currently serving as chief diversity officer for the University of California at San Diego, introduced the theoretical framework during the workshop. I incorporated the theory into the *Anatomy of an Ism* model. It begins by first defining a bias as a preference or proclivity towards something or someone.[28] When we express a bias, we disclose our preferences for one thing over another. Desiring water versus soda is an example of a bias. Choosing Michigan State University over the University of Michigan to win a football game is another example. Usually, our biases are fairly insignificant and unimportant in the grand scheme of things.

THE ANATOMY OF AN ISM

BIAS: A preference or proclivity towards something; A bias discloses our preference for one thing over another. Biases are relatively harmless, insignificant and meaningless in the grand scheme of things and possessing a bias is quite natural. Our biases are often unnoticed or unrecognized. **Examples:** Preferring a Pepsi over a Coke, or Salmon rather than Swordfish.

Beliefs & Thoughts

STEREOTYPE: A fixed, generalization assumption assigned to a group of people typically based upon limited experiences and information and often attributed to individuals who are part of the group to which the stereotype has been assigned. **Examples:** White men can't jump, Asians are good at math, and blacks can dance, are very athletic, especially in basketball.

Attitudes & Emotions

PREJUDICE: Pre-judging an individual or group of people based upon a perceived stereotype. Denotes a relationship between prejudices and stereotypes. If you harbor stereotypical beliefs, chances are you are prejudiced. The major distinction between our stereotypes and our prejudices are the attitudes and emotional energy attached to our stereotypical beliefs. **Example:** Hesitance and reluctance to select the white guy for a pick-up basketball game because of the stereotypical belief that he can't jump.

Actions & Behaviors

DISCRIMINATION: Any action that results in advantaging or advancing some; while disadvantaging or inhibiting others; regardless of merit. A critical component of discrimination most often overlooked is the element of disregarding merit which consequently, results in the utilization of arbitrary or subjective criteria. **Example:** Selecting a white player over a black player for the team even though the black player is much better based upon salient criteria.

Systemic & Systematic

ISM: Refers to an ideology representing the guiding doctrines or beliefs of a group. An "ism" involves the systemic and systematic manifestation of discrimination. The "ism" exists to the extent that the racial discrimination is perpetuated; hence, making it identifiable as a systemic ideology. This "ism" permeates each facet of the community within which it is allowed to exist, often imbedding itself into the culture, and an "ism" is predictable, calculated, and organized. **Example:** Blacks are not selected for any teams in the NBA; slavery, the Jewish holocaust, Apartheid, Jim Crow, and segregation.

Figure 2.

We all possess biases, whether we are aware of them or not.[29] Malcolm Gladwell's book *Blink* supports this belief, as do a plethora of published scholars covering the science of bias. When considered as an isolated incident, biases generally pose no real threat, create no real challenge, and represent no cause for shame or guilt. They are what they are: our preferences. However, our biases can quickly manifest into something far worse than simple preferences. When biases emerge as stereotypes, there is the potential to experience high levels of impact. A stereotype, defined as a generalization about a group of people or individuals, is often formed based upon limited information. The problem with stereotypes is that they are applied to every individual who is part of the group to which the stereotype is assigned. What may hold true, generally speaking, does not necessarily apply to every individual within that particular group.

Dr. Barbara Harro posited in her book, *Teaching for Social Justice*, that our socialization causes each of us to develop in pre-conditioned ways. We form stereotypical views from receiving enormous amounts of stereotypical input. Input that extends beyond formal and informal education and in spite of, or because of, how we were raised.[30] We cannot escape stereotypes unless marooned on an island and raised by primates instead of people.

Consider some of the racial stereotypical exposure you have encountered about those around you during your lifetime.. Many people have heard assertions like:

- "White men can't jump"
- "Asians drive poorly"
- "Mexicans are lazy"
- "Blacks love fried chicken and can really dance"
- "Indians are drunks."

On occasion, we hear statements like, "Asians are good at math" and consider that to be positive. It is still a stereotype and it is not positive because some individuals of Asian heritage struggle with mathematical concepts and require tutorial support. When a teacher or professor assumes a student is good at math, without assessing how that student is really faring, the student may never receive the assistance needed to ensure their success.

When my biases are fueled by beliefs, and those beliefs are based upon limited information specifically related to a group (or individuals associated with a group), my biases manifest as stereotypes. During our early development as toddlers and preschoolers, we begin differentiating between diverse items and people and solidifying our personal preferences. According to Dr. Harro, once socialized to prefer one choice over another, we also learn to stereotype and generalize using limited information.[31]

It's difficult to admit that each of us possesses stereotypical perceptions of others. What's even more difficult is escaping the indoctrination of such stereotypes. So many of us encounter stereotypical thinking during our early stages of development, and we remain too unsophisticated to adequately challenge stereotypical thinking or comments. As a result, we accept at face value what we were taught to believe.

Have you ever found yourself feeling the need to guard against negative thoughts about people based solely upon their race? On some level, this inclination is an indicator of accepting stereotypes. It may become even more challenging to reject stereotypes when someone from another race does something with which you disagree.

The need to police our thoughts serves as a reminder of just how we are influenced by the numerous hours of biased and stereotypical education we receive through media and within our social circles. Each of us possesses stereotypes, and none of us is exonerated. Believe it or not, it is actually liberating to admit that we have them. More importantly, it's essential that we make this acknowledgement. Because as long as we deny the existence of stereotypes within our personal belief systems, we hinder our ability to heal. Our capacity to recover from the impact of stereotypes begins with each of us acknowledging we have those biases.

Next, is the progression from our stereotypes to our prejudices. Prejudice stems from pre-judging an individual or group of people based upon a stereotype. Our stereotypes can easily lead to prejudices. If you possess stereotypical beliefs, chances are you also are prejudiced. Most of us are challenged to admit we are prejudiced because the idea of being prejudiced carries such a negative connotation. Yet, like stereotypes, we can only overcome our prejudices by first admitting they exist.

Each of us possesses prejudicial feelings and attitudes, even on our best days. Regardless of our status in society, formal education, diverse friendships, political affiliation, socio-economic standing, the positions and titles we hold, or the good deeds we perform, there is some amount of prejudice in each of us. Even those activists who fought side-by-side, upholding civil rights and *justice for all,* possessed racial prejudices.

Dr. Harro suggests that our socialization necessitates the very existence of those prejudices.[32] In fact, our racial prejudices can often ignite or incite our commitment to fight for civil liberties. Those who recognize their own racial prejudices work not only to eliminate racial prejudice within themselves, they are also motivated to eradicate racial prejudice within society. Many white and Jewish civil rights supporters realized their own racial prejudices and consequently, the need to fight to minimize the impact of those prejudices nationwide.

We often rely upon our stereotypical views and beliefs to predetermine what a person is like and what to expect from them. At times, we even anticipate what people are likely to do, and maybe even how they will perform, based upon their stereotypes. We make assumptions about who is safe or dangerous because of how we are socialized. Several years ago, researchers at The National Opinion Research Council (NORC) at The University of Chicago conducted a study that revealed eye-opening results regarding people's beliefs about academic superiority and inferiority based on race. The study reported over half of the participants surveyed believed blacks were intellectually inferior to whites.[33]

When we make judgments about people, our judgments carry an assigned value or worth. In order to make those judgments, our beliefs, attitudes and emotions must coalesce in the process. There is an emotional energy involved when we stereotype. Emotions are more difficult to deny than beliefs. We can easily assume we have been influenced by others to think a certain way, but we have to own our emotions. When we embrace a prejudice we engage our beliefs, which may be influenced by our emotions, for which we are 100 percent responsible. Accordingly, we shift from merely believing stereotypical views, to possessing feelings about the stereotypes we have formed.

Because there are so many emotions tied to prejudices, we may have a difficult time admitting how truly prejudiced we are. The progressive transition from stereotypes to prejudices begins when our beliefs energize our emotions. Once our emotions and attitudes become part of the process, we are susceptible to deeper levels of impact upon others and ourselves because the emotional component intensifies the situation. Whereas our simple biases function in a relatively harmless manner, our stereotypes and prejudices carry with them more potential interpersonal relationship potency. The problem occurs within us when our personal biases surface as racial stereotypes and transform into racial prejudices. Each of us is hardwired in much the same way, therefore experiencing similar outcomes.

Defining Discrimination

Defining racism does not end with clarifying racial prejudice. In reality, understanding what racism really means begins by defining racial prejudice. However, racism cannot exist based strictly upon the existence of racial prejudice.

How we feel about each other does not cause meaningful, damaging impact until we act out our feelings of animosity and aggression. Thus, the next step in the anatomy of an ism involves acting upon one's prejudices. When we move from our prejudices towards actively discriminating, we act upon our prejudices.

The Collins English Dictionary defines discrimination as, "Any action that results in giving advantage to or advancing some people, while impeding or inhibiting others, regardless of the merit they possess."[34] A critical component of discrimination that is often overlooked is the element merit. When the merit a person possesses is overlooked, other arbitrary or subjective criteria are used to assign value or worth. Oftentimes, arbitrary and subjective criteria used to judge worthiness stems from our biases, stereotypes and prejudices. When the source of that bias is based solely upon one's racial differences, the result is racial discrimination, or discrimination based upon race. Because race is a mythical dimension of distinction, it possesses no real value, worth or merit.

Differentiation, unlike discrimination, involves the use of merit-based objective criteria to determine how to appropriately categorize, compartmentalize or distinguish between two entities. The need to distinguish and differentiate is crucial in everyday life. We differentiate between apples in super markets, search engines on our laptops, types of toothpaste and hair product, the kind of gas to fuel our cars, the route we drive to work. We do this dozens, even hundreds of times in a day, all for a reason and with a purpose. We make distinctions utilizing key criteria to identify important characteristics or to understand the purpose something serves. Yet, when we discriminate, the purpose served is disregarded and the criteria used become extremely subjective. We then provide advantages to those we prefer, subsequently putting others at a disadvantage.

When racial discrimination is in effect, the perceived assets a person brings to the table is trumped by the value being wrongfully assigned to them through racial association. Racial discrimination creates blinders that hide intrinsic value when considering offering opportunities or granting privileges. Once we assign value to any person's race, rather than other essential attributes, we have assigned value to that which has no scientific proof, no validity, nor any true worth. Remember, if race does not exist, it therefore carries no true merit except that which we arbitrarily and artificially construct.

Racial Discrimination and Racism

The United States possesses a strong, long history of race-based discrimination. Prior to the creation of racial taxonomy, peoples' engagement in discriminatory acts was not based upon racial differences. We discriminated against each other based upon other dimensions of diversity, like sex, language, religion and socio-economic status. Once the idea of race was introduced into the social psyche, disparate treatment for some, and unmerited privileges for others, resulted. Whites learned to discriminate against everybody not considered white. Yet whites were not, and are not, the only ones who learned to discriminate based upon race.

Often, when discussing racial discrimination, we are quick to point to the Jim Crow era, which included the more recent civil rights period of the 1950s and 1960s. Privileged whites were allowed to sit at the front of the bus while blacks were relegated to sit in the back. The creation of Japanese internment camps serves as a prime example of how whites legally discriminated against people of color. Yet we fail to discuss how blacks discriminate against whites based upon race, or how whites and blacks discriminate against Asian, Latino/Chicanos and the native indigenous people of the United States. We don't, and won't, talk about it. Neither do we discuss how Asian, Latino/Chicano and native indigenous people discriminate against blacks and whites based strictly upon race. Worse yet, the subject of how whites discriminate against whites, blacks discriminate against blacks, Asians discriminate against Asians, is also taboo. We pretend that these things never happen, but our history is replete with examples.

When black people make the statement, "I'll never date a white person," and the statement is based solely upon race, the statement represents racial discrimination. The merit of the individual is disregarded. What they bring to the relationship as a person matters not. When an Asian storeowner refuses to serve blacks, assuming they will steal something, that is an example of racial discrimination. Never mind the fact that the young black person may have a six-figure income. When a Hispanic person insists on living in a white neighborhood, rather than among the indigenous people of the US because they are Indians, that is racial discrimination.

The most recent two presidential elections clearly highlight examples of racial discrimination. If any one of us voted for a presidential candidate based upon their race and disregarded merit, we too are guilty of racial discrimination.

One such form of discrimination by blacks against blacks was the brown paper bag test. The origins of the test may be up for debate, but not the fact that various times during the 20th century this test was used to discriminate against blacks whose skin tone was darker than a brown paper bag. In his book, *The Future of the Race*, Dr. Henry Louis Gates Jr. tells how black classmates used the test to determine who would gain access to parties.[35] And in her book, *The Paper Bag Principle: Class, Colorism and Rumor and the Case of Black Washington, D.C.*, professor of African American literature, Audrey Elisa Kerr, wrote of sororities, fraternities, churches, and other social organizations that used this test throughout the 20th century to deny dark skinned blacks membership.[36]

The degrees of racial discrimination range from subtle to blatant. While your average person might not engage in blatant forms of discrimination, each of us is guilty of exercising some level of racial discrimination. I characterize us as equal opportunity discriminators. Our biases lead to stereotypical beliefs, resulting in prejudicial attitudes and emotions that guide us to act out in a discriminating fashion. Each of us suffers from the disease known as racial discrimination. None of us are immune. Even our best efforts to resist our own tendencies toward racial discrimination point us back to our upbringing and the cultural influencers impacting our ideology. We are products of our socialization in inescapable ways.

Although racism cannot exist without racial discrimination, the two concepts are not the same. It is possible for racial discrimination to exist without manifesting into full-blown racism. But racism can only mature as a result of, and in the presence of, racial discrimination. At the point the word "race" acquires the suffix "ism," key elements are already present; elements that cause actions associated with discrimination to operate at a deeper, more pervasive level.

What most people misunderstand is that racism is not about how blatant the act is, nor how intense the bias from one individual towards another. For example, being an extremist does not necessarily make one racist. Nor will having a friend from a race different than your own keep you from being racist. Don't assume that only racists burn crosses, write epithets, use demeaning slurs or spew venomous hatred. These actions have long served as the litmus test for who is considered a racist, but they are not all-inclusive. Based on that thinking, it is easy to conclude Don Imus made racist statements when referring to the 2007 Rutgers women's basketball team as "nappy-headed ho's," whether he intended his reference to be racist or not.[37]

To fully appreciate the precise meaning of racism, we must look beyond the most blatant expressions of racism. We need to burrow deeper into the systems and structures in which those actions and behaviors thrive. For that reason, our best working definition of racism is, "The systemic and systematic manifestation of racial discrimination." This posits that there is a progression from racial discrimination to racism. In order for racism to exist, racial discrimination must be present on some level.

What causes racial discrimination to become racism is the manifestation of racial discrimination on a systemic level and in a systematic manner. There is a distinction between racial discrimination and racism. Not every act of racial discrimination is considered a racist act, unless it operates on a systemic level and in a systematic manner. We need, then, to identify what critical component shifts the "ism" from discrimination to the degree and level where it becomes more broadly perpetuated.

Systemic and Systematic Manifestation

When something operates systemically, it permeates throughout every part, segment, and sector of the organization. When we speak in terms of the systematic manifestation, we're referring to its predictability, calculated reoccurrence and pervasiveness. Whenever racism is present within an institution, it is not by chance. It is orchestrated in an intentional and well-organized manner. The transition from racial discrimination to racism is a slippery slope; therefore, I offer the following example.

Consider this scenario: a Major League Baseball team owner forbids a black player to join the team. When the issue is limited to only one team owner disallowing one black player because of the player's skin color rather than his skill-set, that represents a singular act of racial discrimination. If every team in Major League Baseball followed suit, the act represents full-blown racism, because it operates systemically and systematically within the league. As long as one owner exercises his or her prerogative to disallow a black player to join the team, racial discrimination is merely wrong, yet limited in its impact. Once an owner operates within a system that is set up and designed to marginalize and disenfranchise an entire group of people based solely on race (disregarding merit), racism is born.

Some may ask, because the players of the National Basketball Association (NBA) are predominantly black, does that make the NBA racists? No. The vast majority of owners and coaches are white, and while the majority of players are black, there has been no attempt made to holistically prevent white players, or any other racial/ethnic group, from playing in the league. Players are chosen strictly based upon skills, talents and abilities.

Commissioner Adam Silver's reaction to L.A. Clippers' owner Donald Sterling's racist rants in reference to him not wanting to see his girlfriend accompanied by black men at L.A. Clippers' games speaks to this point.[38] Mr. Silver's response sent a strong message that the NBA would not tolerate such behavior, which went a long way in mitigating the incident. It could be said that he prevented the NBA from being viewed as an agent of systemic racism. By nipping it in the bud, Silver discontinued what most sports agencies had historically perpetuated for prior decades. We have undeniably witnessed much progress, particularly within sports and entertainment.

James Jones echoes multiple social scientists in his statement that "racism results from the transformation of racial prejudice and/or ethnocentrism through the exercise of power against a racial group defined as inferior, by individuals and institutions with the intentional or unintentional support of the entire culture."[39] Jones' statement supports the premise that racism stems from prejudice. I have a slightly different perspective on this premise.

In the *Anatomy of an Ism* model (*See Figure 2*), I state that prejudice relates to emotions and attitudes, not actions. A person can own a negative attitude about another person based upon racial differences, yet do nothing to demonstrate that negativity. If that same person acts out his or her negative attitude with language or physical action, racism is set in motion. A negative attitude set in motion, becomes a behavior that can impede a person's ability to participate, succeed, advance, and function at optimal capacity. Negative behaviors cause major trouble, while unspoken ideologies, opinions and attitudes don't. Albeit the distinction represents a fine line, it's a line that underscores where racism comes from. Racism stems from discrimination rather than prejudice.

Yet, Jones also identifies power as the key ingredient required for racism to operate at a systemic and systematic level. Power fuels an ism. Sociologist Robert Staples defines racism as prejudice plus power.[40] He understood how the presence of power was essential to the existence of racism. Absent power, neither racism, nor any other form of an ism, could exist. When we strip away the power, we are left with acts of discrimination that cannot be instituted at a systemic level. This is the case even when negative actions are premeditated.

In *Playing the Race Card*, Dei, Karumanchery and Karumanchery-Luik maintain, "There is a connection between race and racism in that the term race speaks of power to define, otherize, and categorize. Racism is an outward manifestation of that power."[41] While many 20th Century thought leaders like Jones, Staples, Anna Quindlen, Spike Lee, Joel Kovel, Coramae Richely Mann, Paula Rothenberg and Sister Souljah support that theory, others like Dinesh D'Souza, author of *The End of Racism,* disagree, claiming that blacks too can be racist. He states:

> "If racism requires prejudice and power to exist, and prejudices run through us all, then who wields the most power? Blacks may possess the former, but they do not possess the latter. Very well. If this is true, then it naturally follows that the Ku Klux Klan and the Skinheads are not racist organizations. The Klan and the Skinheads do not sit in the legislature, there are no Klan or Skinhead mayors, they are absent among directors of major corporations, they cannot be found among foundation heads, university faculty, school principals, and the like," [42]

D'Souza adds, "Blacks control the reins of power in many urban areas." Yes, there are 45 blacks in the United States Congress, 43 serving in the House of Representatives and, for the first time ever, two serving in the Senate. And the United States President is black. But the percentage of blacks serving in the 113th US Congress is still only 8.3 percent.[43]

In politics, academia, business, and industry, white men finish first. American college presidents are overwhelmingly white, and getting whiter. The American Council on Education reports that racially or ethnically diverse presidents lost ground in 2011 when the number of black college presidents fell from 13.6 percent in 2006 to 12.6 percent five years later. This included presidents at historically black colleges.[44]

When Microsoft announced in early February 2014 that it had named Satya Nadella, a native of India, as its new CEO, the titans of industry weren't threatened. Thinkprogress' report showed that white men still dominated Fortune 500 companies as CEO positions. There are just six black CEOs, or 1.2 percent of the total Fortune 500 CEO population, even though blacks make up 13+ percent of the overall US population. There are eight Hispanic CEOs, only 1.6 percent of the top business execs nationwide, while Hispanics total nearly 17 percent of the population. Gender diversity hasn't changed in four years. Fewer than 15 percent of Fortune 500 chief executives are women; also disproportionate since women make up half of the US population.[45]

The power differential remains statistically evident. While the number of racially or ethnically diverse people and women within corporate America has increased, the numbers among leadership remain the same, and in some cases, decreased. Since power tips the scale of racial discrimination further towards racism, clearly delineating who possesses power and how power is used crystalizes the argument. It is therefore necessary for us to unpack the element of power and examine the power dynamics at work.

CHAPTER 4

"Race has become metaphorical, a way of referring to and disguising forces, events, classes, and expressions of social decay and economic division far more threatening to the body politic than biological 'race' ever was."
Toni Morrison (1931-) Novelist and Nobel laureate

THE MANIFESTATION OF RACISM IN SOCIETY

Because power is essential in the manifestation of racism, and our country has experienced major shifts in power, it stands to reason that the dynamics of power would have shifted as well. In contemporary times, power is defined by influence rather than brute force. The emergence of Condoleezza Rice, Colin Powell and Barack Obama on the political front beg the question, is racism still a problem in the United States of America? Blacks have made enormous gains. Since Obama's re-election, the blogosphere and media have asked the question: Is there a continuing need for organizations like the NAACP, Urban League and affirmative action programs? Is the power shift in our country proving our efforts to abolish racism are working?

There is a correlation between power and racism. Power allows racism to exist on an institutional level. Joe R. Feagin, a US sociologist, conducted extensive research on racial and gender issues and concluded that race exists systematically.[1] Institutional racism supports and encourages individual racism. Power inherent within any system makes institutional racism possible. Power can allow racially discriminatory practices to operate systemically throughout and across numerous institutions simultaneously. When one group has significant access to power, while other groups have limited access to similar power, imbalances occur.

Defining Power

Power is the ability to decide, determine and choose in ways that impact ultimate outcomes. Power equates to control. Those who are in control possess power, that being the ability to make decisions and influence outcomes impacting communities of people. Power exists in a continuum ranging from contained amounts of power to ultimate/omniscient authority. (*See Figure 2.1*). People with limited power have reduced chances of creating change or controlling outcomes. Those with the power, obvious ultimate/omniscient power, have the ability to create scalable and sustainable change, impacting a large segment of the population.

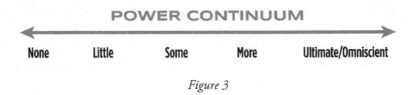

Figure 3

Omniscient power extends far beyond one individual's personal capacity. An individual may have personal power, but unless that power is supported by the overall system that is their universe, the power is rendered irrelevant or insignificant. Personal power allows us to impact the lives of any number of people: children, spouses, extended families, co-workers, neighbors and those in our community. Personal power might allow an individual to influence a company, or even an industry, but personal power doesn't equate to systemic control. For an individual to acquire power at the institutional level, they must first possess hierarchical power. Even then, the individual is still somewhat limited.

When a National Football League (NFL) team owner refuses to allow black players to play for his or her team, the franchise owner possesses personal power and his or her actions impact the lives of a number of potential players. The owner controls his or her respective team, but not the entire league. If the Commissioner of Football were to institute a policy banning any black player from playing for any team in the league, the Commissioner would be imposing the decision on behalf of the entire league. That decision reflects hierarchical power. If the league does not support the decision of the Commissioner, the personal decision of the Commissioner stands little chance of operating across the league, greatly diminishing the Commissioner's power.

Hierarchical power is extinguished the moment a powerful individual relinquishes his or her position. Personal power shows up as a blip on the radar, while hierarchical power can manifest and affect the lives of hundreds, thousands and more. Ultimate power, with its ability to affect the masses or members of an organization, is the only power that can fuel an "ism."

Power within Systems and Institutions

Power is manifested through systems and the institutions orbiting each of those systems. *See Figure 4*

POWER GRID STRUCTURE	
SYSTEMS	**INSTITUTIONS**
Economic	Banks, Businesses (Public and Private)
Educational	Schools, Colleges, Universities
Political	Democrats, Republicans, Independents
Legal/Governmental	Courts, Local, State, Regional, Federal Government and Municipalities
Healthcare	Hospitals, Medical Schools, HMOs
Military	Army, Navy, Air Force, Marines, Coast Guard
Religion	Churches, Synagogues, Mosque
Media/Entertainment	Mass Media, Sports, Studios

Figure 4

Within each system and institution, certain decision-makers emerge. By virtue of their power, these decision-makers make choices affecting the direction, scope, involvement and impact of the entire system or institution. Power this potent is power that is used for the overall institution, not for an individual. When a bank president makes a decision for her bank that affects the bank employees, the rest of the banking sector remains unaffected and the economic system is even less likely to experience any significant changes. When the practices of a single bank are replicated at every bank in the financial sector, the policies, procedures and principles are systemically and strategically manifested throughout the banking system. A person making this level of decision possesses hierarchical positional power as a figurehead of the company.

Enslaved Africans were often used as gatekeepers and enforcers tasked with disciplining fellow slaves. They had no real power because they were only functioning as their master's agents, ordered to manage their peers. In contemporary times, people of color may possess both a title and status that allow them to enforce rules and regulations upon other people. Yet, the majority of people of color do not wield enough power to legitimately control others. Bottom line: rarely do blacks, Asians, Hispanics or native indigenous people possess hierarchal control in the United States.

When we analyze who has hierarchical power netting ultimate control and systemic impact, obvious and undeniable patterns emerge. Who holds the power to make decisions, determining and choosing actions in ways that impact ultimate outcomes, by the numbers and by race? *See Figure 5*

POWER GRID STRUCTURE - RACE

SYSTEMS	INSTITUTIONS	WHO HAS POWER
Economic	Banks, Businesses (Public and Private)	White
Educational	Schools, Colleges, Universities	White
Political	Democrats, Republicans, Independents	White
Legal/Governmental	Courts, Local, State, Regional, Federal Government and Municipalities	White
Healthcare	Hospitals, Medical Schools, HMOs	White
Military	Army, Navy, Air Force, Marines, Coast Guard	White
Religion	Churches, Synagogues, Mosque	White
Media/Entertainment	Mass Media, Sports, Studios	White

Figure 5

In the United States, whites dominate every system and institution. People from racially or ethnically diverse backgrounds may serve in leadership roles within a specific institution. But invariably, they lack enough power to control an entire system. On an individual level, the overwhelming majority of whites don't possess control and cannot make decisions to affect a system or organization. As previously stated, one individual can do very little damage and cause only minor change. Yet, backed by a system or an entire institution, individuals who demonstrate hierarchal power carry significant influence and authority. Because the majority of those in power are white, and whites maintain collective control. Collective control has market share and nets institutional control, resulting in systemic control.

All Racists Are Not Bad People

Not all people in positions of power are personally responsible for creating the dynamic of systemic control. There are plenty of white people who are not responsible for the systems they operate in, nor do they occupy positions of power. Still, they are likely to benefit, even if indirectly, because other whites do sit in those positions. In their defense, they may not have chosen to benefit from the indirect form of power extended to them. In fact, if given the choice, I would like to believe that many whites would prefer to see power redistributed to create greater inclusion. I believe they would welcome extending the power to individuals lacking opportunities, particularly in cases where individuals were deserving of such power. There are absolutely white people that want those deserving of opportunities and promotions to receive them when they have earned them, regardless of race.

You can find countless examples of whites that have worked tirelessly to abolish, eradicate and eliminate racism whenever and wherever they have found it. Still, even the most ardent, anti-racist advocates admit to struggling with their own personal internalized racist ideological indoctrinations. I refer to them as the well-intended, good-hearted people of society who comprehend the true nature of racism and seek to do their own self-work to overcome the impact of racism in their own lives. My desire is neither intended to attack white people, nor blame them for the power they either benefit from or personally possess. I also acknowledge the commitment of many white people who fight diligently to address racial inequity.

When I use the word "racist," I am referring to those persons or groups of people who benefit from a system favoring certain people, while disfavoring others, regardless of credible and objective criteria. Our socialization perpetuates the racist system at work today. It causes the empowered, as a group, to remain in power, while the disempowered, as a group, remains disempowered. Consequently, being labeled a racist does not always mean you are a bad person. Most people who are labeled racist are not bad, mean-spirited, or ill-willed at their core. "Ism," as a suffix, identifies the systemic nature of our social condition. Replace the word "race" with the word "sex," add the suffix "ism" and the focus becomes sexism rather than racism. Like racism, sexism results in the marginalization of women and the advancement of men, regardless of merit. Similarly, many men benefit indirectly from sexism while despising how women are disenfranchised, yet operate as sexists on a daily basis. Men are often unaware of their participation in the perpetuation of sexism. Sexists aren't automatically bad people, especially when their sexist thinking or behavior is unintentional. *See Figure 6*

POWER GRID STRUCTURE - SEX		
SYSTEMS	**INSTITUTIONS**	**WHO HAS POWER**
Economic	Banks, Businesses (Public and Private)	Men
Educational	Schools, Colleges, Universities	Men
Political	Democrats, Republicans, Independents	Men
Legal/Governmental	Courts, Local, State, Regional, Federal Government and Municipalities	Men
Healthcare	Hospitals, Medical Schools, HMOs	Men
Military	Army, Navy, Air Force, Marines, Coast Guard	Men
Religion	Churches, Synagogues, Mosque	Men
Media/Entertainment	Mass Media, Sports, Studios	Men

Figure 6

Replace the word race with the word sex and ask the question, "Who possesses the decision-making power?" within each system and institution. The answer is consistently men, as illustrated in Figure 6. In some cases, numerically speaking, women equal and sometimes outnumber men within the workforce. Still, at leadership levels, men dramatically outnumber women. Too often we hear about women occupying the same position as men and getting paid far less in salary and benefits.

These disparities reflect the reality of sexism in society. In that regard, racism and sexism mirror one another. Though not viewed by academicians as a scholarly reference, I cite *Wikipedia*, which sums it up this way:

"In a similar way to defining racism, sexism can refer also to any and all systemic differentiations based on the gender of a person, not based on their individual merits. In some circumstances the type of sexism described above may constitute sexual discrimination, which in some forms is illegal in some countries."[2]

Like sex, age is an ism that affects our culture. "Ageism" is a term coined in 1969 by US gerontologist Robert N. Butler to describe discrimination against seniors. Butler defined ageism as a combination of three connected elements:

1. Prejudicial attitudes towards older people, old age, and the ageing process
2. Discriminatory practices against older people
3. Institutional practices and policies that perpetuate stereotypes about older people."[3]

In similar fashion, "classism" is considered systemic, prejudicial or discriminatory acts on the basis of socioeconomic class. Classism honors those with status, lineage and title, earned or inherited wealth, education in the traditional sense and exposure to added-value education, like cotillions or other life experiences. There is an advantageous lead on those who don't have access to the same. These are the "haves." When haves enjoy their lot at the expense of the "have nots," classism is divisive. Privileged individuals like those who languished their days away in Fitzgerald's *The Great Gatsby*, for example, assumed that their status and favor was warranted and merited.[4] They failed to perceive any disparity between themselves and the marginalized other half. Blindly, they perpetuated the system.

Racism Manifested

In the United States, political policies, practices, procedures and principles have been based upon racist beliefs. These decisions have allowed certain segments of the population to access power, while others were granted limited or no access to decision-making opportunities. The acts and practices of a few individuals with personal power soon become institutionalized throughout entire systems. At a point in our country's development, the decisions of some individuals permeated entire industries and racism was born. Although the origin of systemic racism occurred several centuries ago, the residual impact remains. We no longer witness overt signs and symbols resembling those of the Jim Crow south, however ample data exists validating the significant disparities between our contemporary citizenry, as mentioned in the previous chapter.

Active vs. Passive Racist

What makes understanding racism more complicated is the notion that all racists are the same, depicted as cross-burning, hate-mongering bigots who spout racial epithets, wear Ku Klux Klan regalia and participate in the vilest of activities. Active, extreme or overt racism remains the easiest to identify. Passive racists exist alongside extremists. Tight-lipped in their commentary and keeping their actions under the radar, passive racists deny access and opportunities to others because of their racial identity. They often do so unknowingly and unintentionally.

Roman Catholic priest Michael Louis Pfleger was chastised in the media when in 2008 he gave a sermon at then-presidential candidate Barack Obama's church, Trinity United Church of Christ. He ridiculed Senator Hillary Clinton, also a candidate for the Democratic nomination, claiming that Hillary was somehow entitled to the presidency because she was white and Bill [Clinton]'s wife. And then, Pfleger added, "along came Obama." Obama's response to Pastor Wright's oration was that he was "deeply disappointed in [his] divisive, backward-looking rhetoric." Pfleger apologized. Obama resigned his membership in the church and the Catholic Church asked Pfleger to take a two-week leave of absence.

Father Pfleger's comments were intended to illustrate to the general public that he was not associated with active racists. In fact, his life-long efforts to abolish racism are notable, both within the church and community at large. On countless occasions, Fr. Pfleger has led non-violent demonstrations in the inner city of Chicago and has been outspoken about racist practices and speech. Yet, he is still considered a "racist" by definition, albeit passive.

As Nathan Rutstein pointed out in his work, *Overcoming Racism*, he identifies himself as a recovering racist and believes overcoming racism, like overcoming alcoholism, involves an ongoing daily process.[5] Recovery occurs one day at a time, even for the most ardent, well-intended individual. I give much credit to Fr. Pfleger and consider him one of my greatest heroes. Be that as it may, I use Fr. Pfleger as an example of one who, if considered racist, is only a passive racist at best, but racist nonetheless.

The stain active racists left upon our nation added to the division between people in the US for centuries. Slavery pitted state against state in the Civil War and inspired civil disobedience in the 1900's. Racism was tolerated, even embraced in the Jim Crow era. And since the dawn of the new millennium, it is just as quickly called out as being unjust. Frowned upon in the court of public opinion, racism now manifests in more subtle or passive forms, and that remains our nation's biggest issue. Passive racism assumes that the status quo needs no improvement. It blurs the line between racial discrimination and racism, while giving a nod to racial discrimination. Passive racism dulls the senses, causing some people to abandon any stand that opposes racism.

Passive racists far outnumber the active racist. As a result, passive racism can leave significantly more collateral damage in its wake than active racism. Although well intended and well meaning, some passive racists are not fans of lifting up a group because of the color of their skin, legacy or marginalized experiences. Some passive racists don't factor in the whole group. They may support the advancement of those who "deserve" to be raised up because they outshine others despite their color; they've overcome the odds.

Black Olympians and athletes, black celebrities and performers, black titans of business, black scholars and academics, black physicians, black political leaders and black ministers—all outstanding people of color—are forgiven their color by passive racists. They are allowed entrée into positions of authority because members of the larger (i.e. white) community judge them as being different, better, worthy of a leg up, or deserving of special considerations not oft afforded most people of color. That's the most damning kind of admission ticket because it comes with a passive racist clause: "You showed us you were better by pulling yourself up by your boot straps. You rose above. You are okay in spite of your race."

Educating passive racists is paramount to eradicating racism. We need to teach passive racists that backing profoundly successful people of color, because they are successful in spite of their race, is potentially as damaging and negatively impactful as the cross-burning, epithet-hurling, aggressive forms of racism. The problem is their passive racism is often steeped in unintentional condescension. Recognizing the impact of their statements and actions represents their biggest challenge. Supporting passive racists in reemerging as recovering, self-reflective, self-directed advocates and allies represents our nation's greatest challenge. However, if we as a nation ever figure out how to positively impact this segment of the population, we will exponentially advance efforts of eradicating, eliminating, erasing and abolishing racism. Therefore, my desire is to focus most squarely upon passive racists, transforming them into self-aware partners committed to trumping the race card.

CHAPTER 5

"We've got to face the fact that some people say you fight fire best with fire, but we say you put fire out best with water. We say you don't fight racism with racism. We're gonna fight racism with solidarity." - Fred Hampton

THE BEHAVIOR AWARENESS MODEL

Nearly fifteen years ago, while employed by ProGroup, Inc., a diversity and inclusion consulting firm, I used the Awareness Spectrum© model to help workshop participants identify how to positively and courageously address inappropriate behavior. The model provided insight and clarity into dealing with problematic situations that were either experienced or observed. While the model got the conversation about racism started, it didn't go far enough.

In its place, I recommend the behavior awareness model, a modified version of ProGroup's plan, developed in partnership with my colleague, Claire L. Tse. We revised ProGroup's model to address racist speech and behaviors. We were cautious about labeling people that engage in racist speech or behavior as "bad people," based on our belief that anyone and everyone could engage in racially discriminatory behavior at some point in their lives. Often speech and behavior are unintentional, not meant to cause harm or injury to others. As discussed in previous chapters, the major distinction between racial discrimination and racism stems from the level of impact racism has in our lives. Because of the systemic nature of racism, whenever it occurs, the ripple effect it leaves behind is broader and deeper than that of a racially discriminatory act. That is not to say that racial discrimination does not possess impact. Quite the contrary: it indeed carries significant impact, if for none other than the individuals involved. Yet, the impact of racism is far more exponential in nature, and the need to retard its progress is all the more essential.

The behavior awareness model depicts the behavior of two types: those who do or say something inappropriate, or who act in inappropriate and racist ways, versus those who witness the inappropriate and racist speech or actions of others. The former operate out of one of four positions: Unaware, Denial, Instigators, or Propagators.

Unaware or In Denial

Individuals who are Unaware, lack experience and exposure. They lack the ability to discern how they misspoke, unable to recognize their own gaffes. Unless an individual is sophisticated enough to comprehend the impact of the racist comment or act, they remain unaware of their contribution to the incident. Once educated, the Unaware person is usually receptive to altering his or her behavior and language moving forward to demonstrate greater respect.

Unlike the Unaware, those in Denial struggle with accepting the problem. Lack of experience, exposure and education makes acknowledging the problem difficult and impairs the ability to understand the root issue. Those in Denial fail to comprehend the rationale behind racism in the first place. If challenged, they typically push back, not because they are mean-spirited but because they struggle to comprehend the true nature of racism. Any resistance they exhibit is rarely malicious or intentional. Their mental and emotional roadblocks result from their lack of experience and socialization. People in Denial assume they have a grasp of the truth and ignore anyone else's interpretation of racism.

In the movie *The Color of Fear*, directed by Lee Mun Wah, eight men engage in intense dialogue about the reality of racism. One of the men, David Christiansen, is a sheltered middle-aged white male who has spent the majority of his life in denial. Ultimately, David grows to understand the experiences of his comrades in the film, and even acknowledges the role he played in perpetuating racism. He admits he was shielded from racist treatment and emerges much more enlightened about racism.[1]

It's a formidable task to enlighten people in Denial. Working to bring about self-awareness may require several conversations over extended periods of time. It's not for the faint at heart, the impatient or insensitive, and it often requires the assistance of a well-informed ally who is willing to patiently guide and educate. In my last chapter, I discuss how essential allies are in supporting those who fail to see where racism exists.

Instigators and Propagators

What distinguishes the Instigator and Propagator from the Unaware or Denial groups is what they do after they receive specific, honest feedback about their inappropriate statements and racist behavior. No matter if the inappropriate behavior is pointed out to them or not, the Instigators and Propagators often operate with malice, ill will and ill intent. They have little regard for what others say or think about them. The only salient distinction between the Instigator and Propagator is related to who starts the ball rolling relative to the racist comment or action. The Instigator creates the email and the Propagator simply circulates it. The world learned during the Holocaust how widespread propaganda sometimes drives exponential damage.

Propaganda spreads for the purpose of promoting some cause. As opposed to impartially providing information, propaganda presents information primarily to influence an audience. Propagators are well aware of the message they spread and the purpose for spreading the message. Instigators benefit from the work of Propagators because the Propagators carry the message and will defend the statements and behavior of Instigators. Both Instigators and Propagators feed on the existence and work of the other. Instigators without Propagators are limited in their ability to impact the masses because Instigators depend upon Propagators to advance their ideologies. Propagators without Instigators, however, have no racist propaganda to carry forward or propagate.

When we encounter Instigators or Propagators, we best serve them by confronting their inappropriate behavior and racist actions or statements by giving specific, direct information about what was said or done and why it was problematic. Most critical is explaining the negative consequences they will experience should they choose to persist their engagement in racist ways.

Education is not what is lacking in the minds or hearts of Instigators and Propagators. They have already chosen to ignore what they know has a negative impact on others. Consequently, they require clearly stated specific consequences imposed upon them to facilitate modification of their speech or behavior. The only incentive to change the actions of an Instigator or Propagator is that which possesses significant impact in their lives. Sometimes, they are only motivated by what hurts them. Therefore, dealing with Instigators and Propagators becomes rather challenging and requires direct action.

We often end up legislating against the behaviors and speech of Instigators and Propagators. But if we litigate and legislate behavior, we should expect to enforce it as well, constantly holding individuals accountable. For that reason, working to raise the consciousness and conscience of people is a far better strategy for altering behaviors than attempting to enforce behavioral change through legislation; although, laws are extremely important towards motivating change. Once people are insightfully enlightened to change their behavior, rather than forcing them to do so, those same people will make concerted efforts to correct themselves, whether they are watched or not. For the Instigator or Propagator, the true desire to change becomes internalized rather than rejected; even deflected.

Those Who Observe

On the other side of the behavior awareness model are individuals who respond to inappropriate behavior when they encounter the racist actions or comments made by others. The respondents did not directly engage in the inappropriate manner themselves. They did not initiate the derogatory speech or actions, yet they did observe what occurred when it happened. There are three types of respondent categories to any racist incident. We either respond as Silent Supporters, Warriors or as Advocates of Change. In each case, how we respond carries significant impact.

The Silent Supporter

A Silent Supporter observes what transpires when a person who is Unaware, an Instigator or a Propagator has spoken or acted in a racist manner. Although the Silent Supporter witnesses the event, their response is reflected in the label. Silent Supporters "see no evil, hear no evil, and speak no evil." Even if the Silent Supporter takes issue with what has occurred, their lack of response breeds assumed consent through their silence. You have probably heard the statement, "Silence breeds consent."

In numerous instances, individuals, groups and institutions have argued that freedom of speech is indeed a constitutional right and deserves to be preserved. Those same people further rationalize silence in the face of offensive behavior by defending the right of every individual to speak as they choose. Understand, however, we can protect a person's right to speak freely while vehemently opposing messages of racism. Leaders are often called on the carpet to render statements countering the positions of hate groups and racists, as well as the intentionally or unintentionally ignorant. In so doing, leaders are expected to take a position and make a stand. Thus, the message can be sent that silently supporting racist acts or speech is just as damaging as the offending act and speech.

Therefore, what Silent Supporters need most is encouragement to take a stand and speak out against the injustice of racists' actions and speech. The root word of "encouragement" is "courage," suggesting that standing up and speaking out requires a significant amount of courage. We find it most difficult to address inappropriate behavior when our supervisors, friends and close associates or respected family members exhibit the offensive behavior. We wish not to be viewed as an outcast, someone who sides with the other group, or an overly sensitive troublemaker. Consequently, we often go along to keep the peace. In reality, we contribute to the damage resulting from racism when choosing not to respond.

When providing encouragement to the Silent Supporter, a successful method of approaching those who engage in racist speech or behavior is equally essential. Silent Supporters often "say and do nothing" simply because they don't know how to address the issue. Providing them with options, coupled with ongoing support, can give Silent Supporters the incentive needed to address racist incidents they witness. Most Silent Supporters are agents of change in the making, needing only the guidance, encouragement and support to address the inappropriate behaviors of others.

The Warrior

The polar opposite of the Silent Supporter is the Warrior, who is always armed and ready to address any racial incident that may arise. The Warrior may even anticipate when racists behavior will occur based on their past experiences and exposure. The Warrior will confront all inappropriate behaviors to prevent the racists' comments or acts from creating damage. Unfortunately, because of the zealous manner in which they address the situation, they may in fact escalate things rather than extinguish them.

Observers of the video, *The Color of Fear*, have often cited Victor Lewis, a participant in the video, as displaying Warrior-type tendencies. Victor, an African American man, reaches a point of extreme frustration in the film when David Christensen, a white male participant, repeatedly denies the existence of racism and discounts the experiences of the other men in the room. Out of extreme frustration, Victor passionately expresses his disdain for David's inability to comprehend the experiences of the other men. Victor's emotionally charged, animated outburst becomes quite loud, he uses numerous expletives and his tone and tenor make David visibly uncomfortable. As a result, David shuts down, withdraws and immediately quits talking for several minutes. To Victor's credit, he did not remain agitated for long. Unfortunately, while he was in his Warrior state, David struggled to remain engaged and to fully appreciate the powerful and poignant message Victor delivered through his impassioned expressions.[2]

Unlike Victor Lewis, what Warriors often overlook is the need to balance passion with compassion. While Warriors are motivated to create change due to the injustices associated with racism, the approach they use leaves those they confront feeling wounded. Often, Warriors are motivated to change the environment because their valid concerns about the racist statement or behavior promulgated by another individual require a response. Yet, the methods used by Warriors can create collateral emotional damage and disengaging reactions. The result is that people often discount and discredit the efforts of a Warrior to address the inappropriate behavior of a person who is Unaware, in Denial, an Instigator, Propagator, or even a Silent Supporter. Because the Warrior assumes people should know better than to engage in such activities, they feel justified in launching an attack against the injustices rendered. While the Warrior is attacking the racist behavior, their passion gets misinterpreted as direct attacks against the racist person.

Warriors need to more effectively respond to racists' acts and speech using key strategies to gain clarity regarding whether or not the offending parties involved understand the impact of their behavior. When Warriors confront the Unaware or those in Denial in the same manner as they would an Instigator or Propagator, the likely response from those they are confronting is fearful withdrawal and immobilization.

Understanding the error of their ways is fairly simple for the Unaware, It becomes more challenging for the Instigator or the Propagator, and fear-invoking for the Silent Supporter as one helps them recognize the need to modify their behavior. When assertively corrected for their speech or behavior, Instigators and Propagators will fight back, while Silent Supports will tuck tail and run. Warriors become most effective when they can balance their passion with compassion, ensuring those receiving the corrective messaging are willing to implement the appropriate, strategic response. When Warriors can successfully alter their approach, they manifests as Advocates of Change.

The Advocate of Change

Advocates of Change understand the necessity of first identifying where people may show up on the behavior awareness model. They then respond in a manner reflecting what each respective person requires in order to modify their own behavior. Because what is most needed by those who are Unaware or in Denial is information and insight, compassionate Advocates of Change respond accordingly. As for the Instigator and the Propagator, Advocates of Change directly address their racist behavior by confirming the negative consequences they will experience if their inappropriate behaviors persist. Even if Advocates of Change do not directly implement the consequences, they make certain consequences are clearly delineated and articulated so Instigators and Propagators have no excuses for communicating a lack of clarity regarding potential consequences.

What differentiates Advocates of Change from Warriors is their communication style. Advocates of Change ensure that Instigators and Propagators understand the potential negative consequences linked to their behaviors. Rather than demanding change and demeaning individuals, Advocates of Change seek first to raise the consciousness of those engaging in racist ways, and then create a learning situation where respectful behavior is self-initiated, instead of imposed or legislated. Advocates of Change use consequences as the last resort, only when all other communication attempts fail to meet intended outcomes. But consequences levied upon Instigators and Propagators must be potent and severe enough to result in a reversal of inappropriate behavior or speech.

Although Advocates of Change, Silent Supporter, and Warriors did not create the racial dynamics we face today, they must respond to racist incidents. Advocates of Change encourage Silent Supporters to take a stance, speak up and address injustices they have witnessed. Understanding the impact of ignoring racists' speech or acts becomes paramount as Advocates of Change enlist Silent Supporters into the process of combating racism. Moral, developmental and emotional support must undergird the efforts of the Advocate of Change to encourage Silent Supporters to advance change. We are much more likely to step into tough conversations if and when we are surrounded by the safety of a support network. Numerous Advocates of Change evolve from Silent Supporters who gain enough courage to address the inappropriate behaviors they see and hear.

Warriors are also potential Advocates of Change in the making. Their transformation occurs as Advocates of Change coach them into employing diverse, effective strategies. What Warriors need most is honest guidance to redirect their passion into productive messaging and relationship building to effect positive change. The more Advocates of Change we develop, the better our chances of combating racism.

CHAPTER 6

"We have talked at each other and about each other for a long time.
It's high time we all began talking with each other."
Bill Clinton, (1946-) US President

TEN STRATEGIES TO TRUMP THE RACE CARD

In poker, a trump card ensures victory. Once a trump card is played, all other cards become irrelevant. In the same sense, a manner of trumping the race card is sorely needed if we as a community, a nation, and a world want to embrace a truly diverse and cosmopolitan community in the 21st century. Unlike a game of cards, by trumping the race card we should not seek to create winners and losers. Instead, the goal should be to build a nation that embodies the tenets of the pledge of allegiance: indivisible, with liberty and justice for all.

One of the most detrimental and reoccurring problems we encounter when we face off against racism is the ability to look the other way. We read our history in textbooks and yet fail to make a contemporary application. Failure to ask the hard questions restrains us from thinking beyond our past and keeps us from moving forward. What plagued us in the past can serve to make us better in the future if we individually and collectively address racism head-on. We owe that to ourselves and our communities. Just as each of us has played a role in the perpetuation of racism, we can each play a part in the eradication of the same. The ten steps to trumping the race card are broad, yet focused on the subject of racism. And I maintain, they are very much so achievable.

Strategy 1: Maintain This Guiding Principle
(The Oneness of Humankind)

The Baha'i faith is credited with supporting the principle of "The Oneness of Humankind," and its application is universal. *In Reclaiming Children and Youth,* Sharon Davis called it the guiding principle behind healing racism.[1] Many religions originating in the eastern and western regions of the world adhere to a belief in the interconnectedness and interrelatedness of all humankind. India Arie sings an interlude stanza from one of her recent cd projects *Testimony, Volume 2,* in which she says, "I'm grateful that you created me from the same grains, from the same things." Inherent in the lyric is this sense of our interconnectedness, because we hail from the same point of origin.

The Book of Acts 17:26 (ASV) states that every nation originated from one. I later learned about the principle of "the oneness of humankind" from one of my favorite professors and colleagues at Michigan State University, Dr. Richard Thomas. A practicing Baha'i and guru on the subject of race and racism, Dr. Thomas informed me of the commitment the Baha'i community maintains to abolish racial inequity around the world. Both he and his wife, Dr. June Thomas, were part of a multi-racial community of believers who genuinely embraced the Bahia principle and endeavored to live out its tenant on a daily basis.

I witnessed how people who were raised in extremely diverse communities, some wrought with historic racial tensions resulting from civil rights residue within Detroit and its surrounding areas, somehow became a community of unified, kindred spirits. Had I not witnessed it firsthand, I would have never believed it humanly possible.

My Christian heritage would have led me to believe I should expect to see racial unity manifested in the Christian church long before seeing it in some other religious community. Supposedly, we are "one in the spirit," according to the hymnologist Peter Scholtes.[2] However, it was Dr. King who said, "We must face the sad fact that at eleven o'clock on Sunday morning when we stand to sing 'In Christ there is no East or West,' we stand in the most segregated hour of America."[3]

I watched Dr. Richard Thomas, with the assistance of his protégé, Dr. Jeanne Gazel, create a campus-based program inviting students to engage in authentic, stimulating dialogue about race and racism. Now in its 10th year, the Multi-Racial Unity Living Experience (MRULE) serves as a staple on the MSU campus, bringing together hundreds of students to explore race and racism in dialogue sessions each week during the academic year. I offer the work of Dr. Thomas and his partner Dr. Gizel, not to entice readers to convert to the Baha'i faith, but to understand how the power of a single principle can manifest as a call to action, impacting countless people in insurmountable ways. I honor the ongoing work of Dr. Thomas and Dr. Gazel and the ripples created by their passionate beliefs.

Strategy 2: Eliminate the Word "Race"

Eliminating use of the word "race" from our contemporary vernacular is easier said than done. Removing any word that has become indelibly engrained in our everyday language from our vocabulary is daunting. Years ago, while attending MSU's Conference on Race, I recall encountering a man who was the first person I heard mention the idea of discontinuing the use of the word "race." I must admit, I considered his idea a bit unrealistic at the time. In retrospect, I realize his premise had merit. Recently, I came across an article written by Adrian Helleman entitled, *What In the World: End Race By Eliminating Racism.* Like me, Helleman based his awareness that there is no scientific proof that race exists as the foundation that it can be eliminated.[4] Words move in and out of use, and some acquire new meaning along the journey. A paradigmatic shift is needed. This shift will be cataclysmic, running through the hearts and minds of each of us. It won't happen overnight. It will require time to allow the shift to sink into our collective psyches and behavioral tendencies.

The word "ethnicity" is a more accurate and befitting descriptor than the word "race." Ethnicity is associated with culture and is more specific than the monolithic expression of race. Within each ethnic group are multiple ways of being. People among the same ethnic groups express a broad and wide range of differences across a spectrum of possibility, while maintaining a common identity in cultural reality. Our ethnicity gives us the freedom to become simultaneously homogeneous and heterogeneous in a way that race prohibits. Imagine what might occur if the time comes that individuals are able to express themselves as they want, rather than through the limiting labels assigned to them? What advantages would a person living between two ethnic identities realize if empowered to express both identities equally, without fear of reprisal or contradiction? Imagine being able to claim, "I'm African-American and Cuban" or "I'm German and Chinese?" The word "race" prevents that, particularly within its contemporary context, because race conjures up a prescribed set of parameters that keep us from experiencing or expressing our true selves.

Avoiding oversimplification is paramount. Simply discontinuing use of the word "race" won't solve our dilemma. Surprisingly, many astute and well-read people are unaware that the word "race" has been systematically eliminated from anthropological textbooks over the past several decades. Alarmingly, the majority of educated individuals have never studied race, nor its concepts and manifestations on society. Moving forward, an aggressive agenda of re-education is due. Our population needs to be informed of the miseducation and myths associated with the outdated concept of race.

If we remove the race card from the deck, we effectively remove the word from our current vernacular. In turn, we eliminate the foundation of racial superiority and racial inferiority in one fell swoop. Any construct that attempts to assert that athletic prowess or academic excellence is connected to race, disintegrates. The focus can then shift from fictitious attributes to fundamental characteristics that successful people share: hard work, determination, perseverance and dedication. None of this can come to fruition until race, as we know it, no longer invokes the negative connotations we currently apply.

Strategy 3: Constantly Assess Who Benefits From Racism

In his book *Uprooting Racism,* Paul Kivel promotes a constant review of current societal inequities and the resulting impact on certain segments of the population. When considering public policy and the allocation of public resources, Kivel asks decision-makers to weigh which issues are addressed, how they are addressed, who gets to participate in the discussion, and what solutions are considered viable.

The response to each is potentially influenced by racism. Kivel asserts these questions should be asked and answered in the educational, economic and political arenas. The answers reveal who really benefits from public policy decisions.[5]

When public policy decisions are made by dominant members of a population, the results will most likely benefit those most closely aligned with the dominant group. The under-represented go unnoticed, unrecognized or overlooked, even in cases when the intent of the dominant group is to benefit the entire community. Racism grants privileges to some groups, while ignoring the negative impact upon less visible groups. The under-represented are likely to need significant additional support because they have been historically marginalized or disenfranchised. We have the best opportunity of reducing the subtleties and micro-inequities associated with race and racism when we address them at the decision making level.

Francis Kendall echoes Kivel's opinion that racism is always operating on some level within society.[6] The majority, white people, don't believe race is a factor. When we don't acknowledge the existence of racism, we grow numb to its subtle influences. Peggy McIntosh's classic article, *Unpacking the Invisible Knapsack,* exposes the invisible privileges alive and well in society based on race.[7] White people don't recognize these advantages as actual privileges. Many white people assume that everybody is treated in exactly the same way. Each individual possesses the same level of access and opportunity, so why create special opportunities for certain groups of people? Invisible privilege prevents whites from asking:

- Who benefits most from public policy decisions?
- How are public schools funded?
- How are court sentences determined?
- Whose work is published first in books and magazines?
- What subjects are taught in schools, and about whom?

White people who believe we live in a post racial society interpret the aforementioned questions as a nuisance, rather than serving as a gauge to measure current societal inequities.

Until we are willing to critically examine our systems through the lens of racism, the likelihood of repeating the same mistakes will increase. We need to take a hard look at how historical and contemporary decisions have shaped our public systems. Once we can admit our decisions affect various segments of society differently, realigning future strategies should follow. For instance, if implementing classes taught in Spanish in certain school districts yields a positive impact on academic proficiency among Spanish-speaking populations, wouldn't it make sense to continue offering English as a Second Language (ESL) as part of the basic public school curriculum?

Strategy 4: Redistribute the Power

Fredrick Douglas made the statement, "Power concedes nothing without a demand." Power is intoxicating. In many ways, the words "power," "privilege," and "access" are synonymous. Racism is predicated on the element of power, so readdressing the imbalance of power and privilege is critical. However, if those who possess power are unwilling to relinquish their power, overcoming racism remains a significant challenge.

Discrimination operates as racism, providing certain individuals or groups with unmerited power, privileges and access, while other segments of the population are limited and restricted. When decisions are made utilizing objective, merit-based criteria, access is equitable. When all things are equitable, we mitigate the risks inherent in operating within imbalanced systems and structures.

We must collectively strategize ways to ensure that all people enjoy equal opportunity; that people who want an education can access education; that all people can be hired into all occupations; that they are equally considered for promotions, are able to hold political positions, acquire housing, and more. Building structures, processes and procedures that utilize equitable, objective criteria for access is possible.

Author Deborah Rosen wrote, "Law was one of the main determinants of women's experiences in Colonial America. Women throughout the colonies lived in patriarchal social systems limiting their autonomy and power."[8] Like blacks and other people of color, women were disempowered. Even today, disparities exist between women's access to power and men's. The imbalances must be corrected. And we must do so while not allowing the redistribution of power to victimize contemporary white men, because they are not responsible for the historical practices still impacting current imbalances.

Access, vis-à-vis merit-based criteria, is the ultimate goal. When women and people of color knock at the door of opportunity and the only thing that is considered salient is gender or race, it is a disservice to humankind. In the recent affirmative action case at the University of Michigan, the supreme court ruled that race could be considered a salient factor. Our racial identity impacts our worldview, our perspectives, opinions and even our contributions. However, racial identity alone does not make anyone more knowledgeable in the classroom or skilled in the workplace. Objective criteria can be used to measure skill and ability. The same criteria must serve as the foundation for access to opportunity for all people.

Redistributing power requires those in power to make certain that those people who have been historically marginalized or disenfranchised no longer experience the same oppressive treatment. Recognizing where great disparities currently exist, coupled with creating effective strategies to redress past practices, will move us towards the proper redistribution of power. That does not mean we should advance or promote people of color at the expense of sacrificing white people. We don't need to reduce standards. We need to be aware that the same merit criteria cannot be applied to all people in the same manner. That would imply that each individual has had the same opportunities and access right from the start. The goal then is to make certain that standards are equitable rather than equal, and that nuances are appropriately weighed and considered.

Strategy 5: Willingly and Openly Talk About Racism

In Aka William's article, Is *Your Baby Racist*, she discusses the work of Bronson and Merryman, the authors of the book *NurtureShock*. In *NurtureShock,* Bronson and Merryman uncover results of experiments conducted by several researchers with both parents and their babies to determine how much bias babies and young children experience in their formative years. The findings were astounding. Researchers found that children display a proclivity for their own racial groups more often than not. Bonson and Merryman share the results of studies by Vittrup, Bigler, and Katz, where each mentions the tendencies of young children to notice and distinguish between their own race and those different from them. Furthermore, the parents were openly and directly disinclined to discuss race or racial discrimination with their children, for fear of creating, rather than mitigating, problems.[9]

According to Bronson and Merryman, in Vittrup's study of 100 white parents, she found that the six parents willing to openly discuss interracial friendships also experienced the most dramatic improvement in the racial attitudes. Bigler believed conversations with children should begin as early as age three, the period by which they have already displayed "in-group favoritism" on some level. And Katz emphasized that the period parents assumed to be the time not to discuss race was the most formidable developmental period in the lives of children. Katz also noted that parents in her study were more comfortable discussing gender differences with their children than racial differences.[10] Unfortunately, in our best efforts to protect and safeguard our children, we sometimes significantly stunt their development.

What Bronson and Merryman prescribed was explicit dialogue between parents and children about race and interracial friendships at the earliest developmental stages of their lives.[11] While scary and challenging, by engaging our children in open, healthy exchanges during the exploratory and inquisitive period of their maturation, I believe we can create advantages for future generations. If we continue along the same vain as previous and contemporary generations, history will no doubt be repeated. One thing is certain; the less openly we talk about race and racial differences, the more mysterious and xenophobic we remain.

I am always intrigued by the power of pairing people in racially diverse dyads during my workshops to discuss their personal stories about race. Whenever dyad partners begin to share their individual experiences with the entire group of participants, the group instantly bonds, experiencing a willingness to both share and listen to everyone's personal stories. On many occasions, those preliminary exchanges have marked the formation of authentic friendships.

Chartering into deeper territory during workshops becomes less threatening based upon the ability of the group participants to transcend beyond the initial vulnerable stage of speaking openly about race. The more frequently we invite and encourage people to do so during the regular course of the day, the easier it becomes for our citizenry. Consider what might happen within your work environment, your school, church or community if you regularly discussed how you were doing regarding race within your environment? What is working well? What could be better? My direct experiences have taught me that the more frequently the dialogue occurs, the more comfortable the participants become. I believe Howard Schultz, CEO of Starbucks, was attempting to do just that with his #racetogether initiative and I applaud him for his efforts.

I also applaud and highly recommend the work of Michael Baran, an anthropologist, and Michael Handelmann, a software game developer, who teamed up to create an app called *Who Am I* and a web-based game entitled *Don't Guess My Race.* The app was developed specifically to encourage parents to engage their children in conversations about race using both a fun and developmental approach. It serves as an excellent catalyst for introducing the idea of race to children in a healthy, non-threatening manner. While players are having fun, the developers infused into the experience interesting facts about race for educational purposes. You can find the link to the game, *Don't Guess My Race,* by visiting www.dontguessmyrace.com/demo/thelearnersgroup.

Strategy 6: Form Alliances Across Ethnic Groups

Part of our historical issues of overcoming racism result from treating racism as a problem isolated to white people. Persons of color often discuss their fatigue associated with attempting to educate whites about racism, both in regards to their own personal experiences and the numerous ways racism shows up in everyday life; ways that often go unnoticed by those in the white community. Blacks, Asians, Pacific Islanders, the indigenous people of this continent and Hispanics who do not identify as white, often view white people as the indirect historical progenitors of racism, although they are not directly responsible for their ancestor's behaviors or decisions. Whites are also at times unwilling to or incapable of understanding their role in perpetuating contemporary racism. As long as no effort is made to bridge the gap between whites and people of color, very little will ever change to enhance relationships across differences. Creating allies, however, can help bridge the gaps between groups, especially in instances like those previously mentioned.

The simple definition for "ally," according to *Merriam Webster*, is "A person or group that gives help to another person or group."[12] White allies are identified as "Those members of the dominant culture in the United States, who actively resist the role of the oppressor, and who act as allies of people of color. Historically and currently, there are white people who engage in antiracist activities.[13] Allies function best to eradicate racism when working to establish equitable environments, because allies understand the necessity of using their power, limited or enormous, to empower the disempowered.

The most effective allies, those who often create the most significant, positive impact, first originate from the empowered community, recognizing their connection to the power conglomerate. They don't deny their affiliation or association with the empowered group. Instead, allies recognize how their identity and affiliation can best serve them when attempting to educate those from their respective group to better understand what they fail to see or comprehend. Even if the person serving as an ally possesses neither a title, nor any true authority, they are aware of the entitlements tied to their identity via their group affiliation. Their willingness to bring racism to the attention of those who remain oblivious to power imbalances serves as an example of how allies operate on behalf of the disempowered.

Within corporate settings, allies serve as leaders who provide access to those previously denied visibility within the upper echelon of the organization. I have watched numerous white men and women create access to interviews, sports tryouts, meetings, events, and promotions at both formal and informal gatherings for people of color. In the world of sports, allies like Branch Ricky proved vital to Jackie Robinson. He modeled for the Brooklyn Dodgers how true allies must willingly risk their own reputation, career and even physical safety for the sake of supporting those to whom they're connected. Once Rickey stepped up to the plate as an ally, Pee Wee Reese and other teammates of Robinson followed suit. As a result, blacks were able to integrate into the game of professional baseball with some semblance of support. Within legal circles, Morris Dees serves as a role model of how allies function.

During the Civil Rights era, countless Jewish individuals and enlightened whites served as allies of the black community, facing the hurtful, venomous speech and actions of white antagonizers. Dr. Beverly Tatum mentioned how allies like Viola Liuzzo and Michael Schwerner, as well as other white martyrs, lost their lives in the struggle against racism.[14]

While some white people have laid their lives on the line to passionately oppose racism and oppression, being a true ally addressing the injustice of racism can be tricky business. Some allies possess positive intentions, yet unknowingly and negatively affect the very people they desire to support. Keith Edwards writes concerning how well intended social justice allies can harmfully perpetuate the very system of oppression they seek to alter.[15]

Chamblee, Kendall and Scott raised a crucial caution while presenting at the National Conference of Race and Ethnicity (NCORE) in 2010. They suggested that being an ally is "not something one does to *help* someone else or to help a group."[16] Some allies seek to be such out of a sense of guilt because of the privilege they experience within society based upon their race. When being an ally emulates from a missionary mindset, the premise complicates the process. The greatest enemy of an ally is allowing defensiveness to get in the way of serving as a true advocate. When allies become defensive, they can potentially derail any progress made and any goodwill extended.

Chamblee, Kendall and Scott also make the distinction between serving as an ally for an individual verses serving as an ally for a particular issue. When serving as an ally for people, forming an authentic relationship becomes the primary focus. The ally seeks to support the individual while engaging in the true work of an ally. Unless an authentic bond is established between the ally and the individual, any attempt made by the ally becomes suspect. Allies of issues, however, focus their energy upon acquiring higher degrees of competency around the "complexities of the issue," insuring their actions result in institutional change.[17] The ultimate goal of the ally of an issue is to establish transformative impact, thereby creating change for individuals as well.

A checklist originally developed by John Raible in 1994 and modified by Kathryn Russell at SUNY, Cortland in 2001, was designed to aid allies in uncovering how their intent might not align with their desired impact. Raible used a Lickert scale to collect individual responses to self-assessment questions concerning their effectiveness as an ally. The assessment included questions like, "I support and validate the comments and actions of people of color and other allies, but not in a paternalistic manner!" and "I have been told I act in a racist manner without knowing it, but I think I'm being an ally." Questions like these remind potential allies of possible landmines to avoid along the journey.[18]

People of color working with white allies must grant them grace to struggle through the process of learning on the job. Acting as an ally requires enormous work on the part of those whites that are courageous enough to willfully assume responsibility for their own development. Unless people of color lay aside the fatigue endured by serving as educators for naïve whites, the chances of whites experiencing personal epiphanies are slim to none. Unfortunately, eradicating racism in the US cannot occur without white allies grabbing the mantle and driving change within institutions across the nation. And white allies will never succeed without the guidance, nurturing, support, and patience of people of color.

Strategy 7: Continuously Educate Yourself

One of the greatest assumptions preventing resolution of racism is that white people are the only ones requiring education about racism reduction. Ask anyone—white, black, Hispanic, or other—to define the word "racism" and you'll quickly discover most people in the United States are short on knowledge about racism. While whites are often more oblivious to the reality of racism and miss both the blatant and subtle manifestation of racism in society, plenty of people in general lack an academic understanding of racism.

As a society, we have arguably worked diligently to address the most blatant acts of racism, yet the more subtle forms of racism continue to plague us. The signs, symbols and symptoms of racism are inextricably woven into the cultural fabric of our society. Racism has the greatest capacity to wreak havoc on the complacent and apathetic. Attempting to rationalize how much better off blacks are today, or how much progress blacks have made, is deceptively dangerous. Yes, we get some credit for strides made like electing a black president in 2008 and 2012. However, these successes can quickly become failures unless we implement an aggressive self-education process whereby each individual can examine their own role in perpetuating racism. The more racially astute among us remain sensitized to the presence of racism. Consequently, they have the ability to spot racial issues before they become explosive. But spotting issues won't guarantee positive outcomes; relevant education will.

Recently, I established a consulting relationship with a client who acquired a grant from a foundation specifically to address potential racial inequity practices, processes, and procedures within the organization's structure. I admired the organization for courageously undertaking such an endeavor. I knew when they became a client that focusing on race would render them vulnerable and volatile, both within the organization and within the community they served. The demonstrated commitment of the CEO, coupled by the support of the board of directors, led the organization to begin the process of organizing an innovative focus group for an information gathering session that successfully uncovered their greatest challenges.

After engaging in the discovery stage, the organization was able to develop a strategic playbook for transforming their entire approach to serving clients and supporting employees. Toward that end, they plan to explore where racial inequities exist and how racial inequity is manifested within the policies, practices, and operational procedures of the overall organization. When companies and institutions commit themselves to engaging in this process, they set themselves up for long-term success.

Strategy 8: Seek to Become Culturally Responsive

The new buzzword among the diversity awareness circles is "culturally competent." Herein is the problem: becoming culturally competent is not easily achieved. As a nation, we are still confused about how best to refer to a black person. "Do I call you 'black' or 'African-American' or 'person of color' or 'brotha' or 'sistah'?" If you're not careful, you might offend someone by using terms incorrectly. On the other hand, if you are black and call into question the term someone else uses to identify you by race, you could be accused of playing the race card.

Offending somebody based on his or her race or racial identity is virtually guaranteed. It will happen regardless of how much experience or exposure we have with people from different ethnic communities. Even if we are prompted to say one thing to a person from a specific ethnic group, the same phrase may not apply to another person from that same ethnic group. What is the right thing to do in that instance? I offer the suggestion of a former colleague; seek to become culturally responsive rather than culturally competent. Accept the fact there is absolutely too much to know about every difference in the world and none of us will ever know all there is to know as it relates to ethnic and cultural differences. We can only use what knowledge we have as appropriately as we are able.

Contrary to popular belief, all black people do not appreciate being referred to as "African American." For others, the term "black" is offensive. Referring to every person of Asian descent as "Asian" can also be considered offensive, especially when that person prefers being referred to as a Pacific Islander. Some people of Mexican heritage would much prefer being called "Chicano," rather than "Mexican" or "Hispanic."

Although the book, *Kiss, Bow or Shake Hands* was a best seller in 2006, the lengthy volume of culture norms falls short of serving as the exhaustive cultural bible for appropriate cross-cultural social interactions. Even if you were to master the material contained within the voluminous work, you would invariable offend someone in some manner. When an unintended offense occurs, the best response involves an acknowledgement of its impact, followed by questions directed to the person regarding how to best interact with them in the future. Never assume what holds true for one individual, will hold true for every person affiliated with his or her community. For further insight, read the most recent literature on cultural dexterity.

Strategy 9: Use Other Forms of Isms to Inform

Each person in the US has experienced some form of discrimination based upon a characteristic difference or dimension of diversity they possess.[19] Women routinely encounter sexism, those under 30 or over 60 years of age have experienced ageism, and Jews are intimately familiar with anti-Semitism. Not every form of discrimination operates at a systemic or systematic level, however all of us know what it's like to be marginalized, disenfranchised, overlooked and mistreated despite our skills, talents, abilities, capabilities and contributions.

When conducting seminars in the past, I have asked participants to consider a time when they were treated differently and to then discuss with a partner the resulting impact upon their performance, level of comfort and confidence. Regardless of who is in the audience, everyone has a story to share with their partner about a situation that impacted them negatively.

Paul Kivel reminds us that while our parallel experiences may differ, they are related on some level.[20] When I encounter negative treatment, I use the feelings, thoughts, and behaviors that surface within me to provide insight into how others who experience negative treatment might have been impacted. Their reasons may be different than my own, but are equally as impactful just the same. Somehow, getting in touch with the thoughts and feelings associated with my own experiences heightens my sensitivities of how others might feel under similar situations. Those same feelings make it possible for me to better understand how an "ism" can impact a person who has been victimized by them.

In some instances, as a result of being victimized and marginalized by sexism, white women have expressed a level of sensitivity concerning the impact of racism to a greater degree than white men. Homosexual men can often better understand the reality of racism based upon their experiences with homophobic degradation. What made Jewish people available to serve as the primary allies of the civil rights movement was their direct experiences with the atrocities of the holocaust during World War II. Once the bug of intolerance, hatred and desolation has bitten people, their ability to associate their own pain with those undergoing similar problems is heightened.

Therefore, it is important for each of us to get in touch with our experiences of marginalization and depravation and to then use those experiences as companion experiences to help sensitize our hearts and minds to what others may undergo in similar situations. The first step in removing our blinders and barriers is simply to "walk a mile in the moccasins of another person."

Strategy 10: Extend and Restore Trust

Racism results in division, and division stifles dialogue. Ironically, the only way to resolve division is through dialogue. Open and honest communication is essential, and it is only possible with trust. It's predictable that we can probably have our most candid dialogue when trust is established. When trust is in question, authentic dialogue cannot occur and our ability to overcome our history of racism remains stagnant.

Stephen M.R. Covey has taught me more about the importance of trust than any other contemporary author or thought leader of our time. Before actually meeting Stephen, I was a disciple of his work and used his books and CDs to educate leaders across the globe about the criticality of trust. Covey refers to trust as "the multiplier" that leads to organizational success.

In the book, *The Speed of Trust*, Covey presents 13 behaviors people must employ to acquire the trust of another individual or group and to restore trust when trust has been lost.[21] I believe by working to extend and restore trust, we can overcome the tense divisions that funereally plague our society. While all are salient, there are four I consider most essential in extending and restoring trust.

In a private conversation, Covey shared with me that the 13 behaviors are actually presented in reverse order. He considers the last one as most essential. Therefore I begin with the 13th behavior:

Listen First.

In the Prayer of St. Francis, he prays; "Oh divine Master, grant that I may not seek to be understood as to understand."[22] As I utter that prayer every morning, I am reminded of the Covey Behavior that admonishes me to listen first. The ultimate goal of a fractured community or a broken relationship suffering from the residue of racism is reconciliation. The step towards reconciliation involves listening first.

The question arises, if both parties are to listen first, who begins the dialogue? I would suggest allowing the person who is least empowered in the relationship to begin the dialogue, promoting the person most empowered to listen first. Extending trust often begins by relinquishing power. By simply allowing the less empowered person to speak first, we can model our desire to truly reconcile our issues.

The second behavior I offer is listed as Covey's 2nd behavior:

Demonstrate Concern.

They key component in demonstrating concern involves showing respect.[23] I have often heard people say respect should be earned. I wholeheartedly disagree. Trust is earned and respect is deserved. Every human deserves to be respected, whether we know him or her or not. When respect dissipates, dialogue disintegrates. Even when we do not agree, maintaining the highest level of respect remains possible. And even more importantly, you do not have to like me to respect me. As humans, we possess the capacity to respect each other regardless of our feeling towards one another.

The third behavior offered is Covey's 8th behavior:

Confront Reality

When we have made efforts to listen first and we demonstrate respect, we can delve more deeply into the heart of the matter. Covey suggests in his work the need to take issues head on, even the undiscussable and tough ones.[24] We can only restore trust by tackling the tough stuff. Reconciling racism will never occur while remaining in surface-level dialogue. No doubt, doing so will create some level of discomfort and vulnerability. Communities of people who come to the table of dialogue, capable of sharing their reality from their respective perspectives, stand the greatest chance of closing the chasm of racial divide between them. The deeper the dialogue, the greater the discovery. And the greater the discovery, the better the recovery.

Finally, I offer Covey's 4th behavior:

Right Wrongs

Covey says when righting wrongs, we must be willing to make restitution when possible and apologize quickly.[25] President Bill Clinton, when in office, extended a public apology to the nation for slavery. I admit, I appreciated the gesture, though I felt President Clinton could not assume responsibility for something he did not create. He neither owned slaves, nor did he contribute to the development of the chattel slave industry.

When we seek to right wrongs, we assume responsibility for that which we are responsible. Unfortunately, I can never apologize for something I did not do, although I may empathize with those victimized by wrongdoing. I can only apologize for what I have done.

That being said, while I would never expect any white person to apologize for the actions of his or her ancestors, I would hope for white people to take responsibility for the manifestation and perpetuation of slavery they engage in today. I realize that I too participate in the manifestation and perpetuation of aspects of racism today, and for that, I apologize. While I strongly believe my role in the manifestation and perpetuation of racism varies drastically from that of white people, I assume some responsibility nonetheless.

As we endeavor to overcome the ills and residue of racism that continue to plague us even centuries later, I invite my readers to the table of dialogue in hopes of it propelling us toward reconciliation. I hope my work has provided us with a more informative framework to guide our discussion. While we still may not agree, at least we can come to the table with a chance to react to the presented information, instead of simply allowing our emotions to fuel the conversation. I look forward to hearing from you and stand prepared to work collaboratively to create an authentic community with you as my partners. Trumping the race card will only happen with us working together.

AFTERWORD

Writing *Trumping the Race Card* has been, simultaneously, a labor of love, a source of frustration, and an encouraging endeavor. A labor of love because after nearly two decades of working in the areas of diversity, inclusion, and race relations, even though the subject matter by its very nature is challenging to traverse, I have developed an abiding and passionate belief that through thoughtful dialogue, individuals can make a profound impact in how we view and come to appreciate one another's differences.

The process of writing *Trumping the Race Card* has proven to be a source of frustration because it required patience I didn't know I possessed. It was my years of training and facilitating that provided me with the firsthand accounts and knowledge that made me feel prepared and qualified to write on the subject matter. Once I began the process of writing, however, life happened and my patience was tested time and time again as my estimated time of completion stretched well beyond my initial date. Interestingly enough, it would be events from those unplanned for years that provided unfortunate realizations as to why more work was needed in the area of race relations and how this contribution to the literary landscape was necessary.

While I was slowly completing *Trumping the Race Card,* we have witnessed the nationally exposed and racially charged events surrounding Trayvon Martin's death, Clipper's owner Donald Sterling's antics, the aftermath of Michael Brown's shooting in Ferguson, and the demise and rebirth of Paula Deen's cooking empire. Each incident has been charged with undertones of racism and viewed against the backdrop of what some have referred to as a post-racial era, marked by two landslide elections of our country's first black president, President

Barrack Hussein Obama. The juxtaposition of these realities represent glaring reminders of how far we have and have not come.

In writing *Trumping the Race Card,* I became acutely aware of, and encouraged by, my belief that the only way for us to trump the race card and render it useless is for us to continue having respectful dialogue about the challenging complexities surrounding the topic of race. To that end, I am happy to have laid my cards on the table and I invite you to do the same by visiting the trumptheracecard.com website. I invite you to ask questions, share your stories, offer solutions and equally important, to listen. Listen to the voices that don't sound like yours, from people who don't look like you, who harbor perspectives that differ from yours. If you can succeed in doing it there, you can succeed in doing it in your day-to-day life and be a part of bringing us one step closer to trumping that race card.

NOTES

CHAPTER 1

[1] P. McIntosh, P. *White Privilege: Unpacking the Invisible Knapsack* (1992), 30-36.

[2] Frances Kendall, F. *Understanding white privilege: Creating Understanding White Privilege: Creating Pathways to Authentic Relationships Across Race.* (Routledge, 2012).

[3] Lee Gardenswartz and Anita Rowe, *Diverse Teams at Work: Capitalizing on the Power of Diversity* (SHRM, 2001).

[4] "2008 Presidential Election," US Electoral College, http://www.archives.gov/federal-register/electoral-college/2008/election-results.html.

[5] "2008 Presidential Election," US Electoral College, http://www.archives.gov/federal-register/electoral-college/2012/election-results.html.

[6] Adam Nagourney, "A Defiant Rancher Savors the Audience That Rallied to His Side," *New York Times*, April 23, 2014.

[7] Irving DeJohn and Helen Kennedy, "Jeremy Lin Headline Slur Was 'Honest Mistake,' Fired ESPN Editor Anthony Federico Claims," *New York Daily News*, February 20, 2012.

[8] Abby Phillip. "Zendaya Blasts 'Fashion Police' Host Giuliana Rancic's 'Ignorant' Red Carpet Diss." *The Washington Post*, February 1, 2015.

CHAPTER 2

[1] "Census 2000 Data for the State of Vermont." US Census Bureau. http://www.census.gov/census2000/states/vt.html.

[2] Trevor Wilson,. *The Human Equity Advantage beyond Diversity to Talent Optimization.* Toronto, ON: Jossey-Bass, 2013.

[3] Ibid.

[4] Alexander W. Astin, "Making Sense Out of Degree Completion Rates," *Journal of College Student Retention: Research, Theory and Practice* 7, no. 1 (2005): 5-17.

5   George D. Kuh, "The National Survey of Student Engagement: Conceptual and Empirical Foundations," *New Directions for Institutional Research* 2009, no. 141 (2009): 5-20.

6   James K. Harter, Frank L. Schmidt, and Corey LM Keyes, "Well-being in the Workplace and its Relationship to Business Outcomes: A Review of the Gallup Studies," *Flourishing: Positive Psychology and the Life Well-Lived* 2 (2003): 205-224.

7   Trevor Wilson, *The Human Equity Advantage beyond Diversity to Talent Optimization* (Toronto: Jossey-Bass, 2013).

8   Ibid.

CHAPTER 3

1   "Racism," Oxford English Dictionary, http://www.oed.com/view/Entry/157097?redirectedFrom=racism#eid.

2   "Racism," Merriam-Webster Online. http://www.merriam-webster.com/dictionary/racism.

3   Macquarie dictionary

4   Audrey Smedley, *Race in North America: Origin and Evolution of a Worldview* (Boulder, CO: Westview Press, 2007).

5   Dave Unander, *Shattering the Myth of Race: Genetic Realities and Biblical Truths.* (Valley Forge, PA: Judson Press, 2000).

6   Michael L. Blakey, "Scientific Racism and the Biological Concept of Race." *Literature and Psychology* 45, no. 1-2 (1999): 29-43. An overview and critical discussion of the origins and history of racial science from Linnaeus to the 1990's.

7   Johann Friedrich Blumenbach and others, *Anthropological Treatises of Blumenbach and Hunter.* (Anthropological Society of London, 1865).

8   *Race: The Power of an Illusion - The Differences Between Us.* (California Newsreel, 2003).

9   *Skin Deep: The Science of Race.* (Canadian Broadcasting Corporation, 1995).

10 Marshall Segal," All of Us Are Related, Each of Us Is Unique [Department of Genetic Anthropology, Geneva, Switzerland]," All Related Syracuse, 2002. http://allrelated.syr.edu/index.html.

11 Clarence Page, "Thanks for Being Honest, Jimmy 'The Greek'-too Honest," *Chicago Tribute*, January 20, 1988.

12 Richard Herrnstein and Charles Murray, *The Bell Curve: Intelligence and Class Structure in American Life* (New York, NY: Free Press, 1994).

13 "A Class Divided," Frontline, 1985. http://www.pbs.org/wgbh/pages/frontline/shows/divided/etc/view.html. A film about Jane Elliott

14 Audrey Smedley, *Race in North America: Origin and Evolution of a Worldview* (Boulder, Colo.: Westview Press, 2007).

15 Ibid.

16 John Tehranian, *Whitewashed: America's Invisible Middle Eastern Minority* (New York, NY: New York University Press, 2009).

17 "History," United States Census Bureau, https://www.census.gov/history/www/faqs/demographic_faqs/when_was_the_first_census_in_the_united_states.html.

18 "Race." United States Census Bureau. https://www.census.gov/topics/population/race/about.html.

19 Audrey Smedley, *Race in North America: Origin and Evolution of a Worldview* (Boulder, CO: Westview Press, 2007).

20 "Indentured Servants in the US," History Detectives Special Investigation, http://www.pbs.org/opb/historydetectives/feature/indentured-servants-in-the-us/.

21 David Kennedy, Elizabeth Cohen, and Thomas Bailey, *The American Pageant*, 14th ed. (Wadsworth Publishing, 2008).

22 "Indentured Servants in the US," History Detectives Special Investigation, http://www.pbs.org/opb/historydetectives/feature/indentured-servants-in-the-us/.

23 Ibid.

24 Audrey Smedley, *Race in North America: Origin and Evolution of a Worldview* (Boulder, CO: Westview Press, 2007).

25 Larry Adelman, "Race: the Power of an Illusion," PBS, http://www.pbs.org/race/000_General/000_00-Home.htm.

26 Thomas Jefferson, "Notes on the State of Virginia," The Federalist Papers Project, http://thefederalistpapers.integratedmarket.netdna-cdn.com.

27 Dave Unander, *Shattering the Myth of Race: Genetic Realities and Biblical Truths* (Valley Forge, PA: Judson Press, 2000).

28 Marriam-Webster Dictionary.

29 Malcolm Gladwell, *Blink: The Power of Thinking without Thinking.* (New York, NY: Little, Brown and Company, 2005).

30 Barbara Harro, "Cycle of Socialization," in *Teaching for Diversity and Social Justice*, ed. Maurianne Adams, Lee Anne Bell, and Pat Jones (New York: Routledge, 2007).

31 Ibid.

32 Ibid.

33 "How Do Americans View One Another? The Persistence of Racial/Ethnic Stereotypes," Diversity Digest, http://www.diversityweb.org/Digest/W98/research2.html.

34 Collins English Dictionary.

35 Henry Louis Gates, Jr. and Cornell West. *The Future of the Race.* (New York, NY: Random House, 1996).

[36]   Audrey Elisa Kerr, *The Paper Bag Principle: Class, Colorism & Rumor and the Case of Black Washington, D.C.* (Univ Tennessee Press, 2006).

[37]   Ryan Chiachiere, "Imus Called Women's Basketball Team 'nappy-headed Hos'" Media Matters, 2007, http://mediamatters.org/research/2007/04/04/imus-called-womens-basketball-team-nappy-headed/138497.

[38]   "Silver: Clippers Owner Sterling Receives Lifetime Ban, Fine for Racist Comments," Fox Sports, 2014, http://www.foxsports.com/nba/story/donald-sterling-punishment-clippers-lifetime-ban-fine-racist-comments-adam-silver-042914.

[39]   James Jones, *Prejudice and Racism.*)McGraw-Hill Companies, 1997), 117.

[40]   Robert Staples, *Introduction to Black Psychology.* (McGraw-Hill, 1976).

[41]   Nisha Karumanchery-Luik, George J. Sefa Dei, and Leeno Luke Karumanchery, *Playing the Race Card: Exposing White Power and Privilege* (Peter Lang International Academic, 2005).

[42]   Dinesh D'souza, *The End of Racism: Principles for a Multiracial Society* (New York: Free Press, 1995).

[43]   Jennifer Manning, "Membership of the 113th Congress: A Profile," Congressional Research Service, 2014, https://www.senate.gov/CRSReports/crs-publish.cfm?pid=%260BL%2BR\C%3F%0A.

[44]   Bryan J. Cook, "The American College President Study: Key Findings and Takeaways," American Council on Education, http://www.acenet.edu/the-presidency/columns-and-features/Pages/The-American-College-President-Study.aspx.

[45]   Lauren C. Williams, "Google's Diversity Report Confirms the Company is Still Dominated by White Men," Think Progress, 2014, http://thinkprogress.org/economy/2014/05/29/3442514/google-diversity-report/.

CHAPTER 4

[1]   Joe R. Feagin, *Racist America: Roots, Current Realities, and Future Reparations* (New York: Routledge, 2001).

[2]   Wikipedia.

[3]   "Legacy of Dr. Robert N. Butler," Columbia Aging Center, http://aging.columbia.edu/about-columbia-aging-center/legacy-dr-robert-n-butler.

[4]   F. Scott Fitzgerald and Matthew J. Bruccoli, *The Great Gatsby* (New York: Scribner, 1996).

[5]   Nathan Rutstein, *Healing Racism in America: A Prescription for the Disease* (Whitcomb, 1993).

CHAPTER 5

[1]   *The Color of Fear.* 1994, http://www.stirfryseminars.com/store/.
[2]   Ibid.

CHAPTER 6

[1]   Sharon E. Davis, "The Oneness of Humankind," *Reclaiming Children and Youth* 18, no. 4.

[2]   Peter Scholtes, "They'll Know We Are Christians," Hymnary, 1966, http://www.hymnary.org/text/we_are_one_in_the_spirit.

[3]   Dr. Martin Luther King, Jr., "Remaining Awake through a Great Revolution," Speech, Live Speech, Washington, D. C., March 31, 1968.

[4]   Adrian Helleman, "End Racism by Eliminating Race," What in the World, 2012, http://hellemanworld.blogspot.com/2012/07/end-racism-by-eliminating-race.html.

[5]   Paul Kivel, *Uprooting Racism: How White People Can Work for Racial Justice* (New Society Publishers, 2011).

[6]   Francis E. Kendall, *Understanding White Privilege: Creating Pathways to Authentic Relationships Across Race*, (Routledge, 2012).

[7]   Peggy McIntosh, "White Privilege: Unpacking the Invisible Knapsack," Institute for Social Research University of Michigan, 1989, https://www.isr.umich.edu/home/diversity/resources/white-privilege.pdf.

[8]   Deborah Rosen, "Women and Property Across Colonial America: A Comparison of Legal Systems in New Mexico and New York," *The William and Mary Quarterly* 60, no. 2 (2003): 355-81.

[9]   Po Bronson and Ashley Merryman, *NurtureShock: New Thinking about Children* (New York: Twelve, 2011).

[10] Ibid.

[11] Ibid.

[12] "Ally," Merriam-Webster. http://www.merriam-webster.com/dictionary/ally

[13] Wikipedia.

[14] Beverly Daniel Tatum, "Teaching White Students about Racism: The Search for White Allies and the Restoration of Hope," *Teachers College Record* 95, no. 4 (1994): 462-76.

[15] Keith E. Edwards, "Aspiring Social Justice Ally Identity Development: A Conceptual Model," *NASPA Journal* 43, no. 4 (2006): 39-60.

[16] Marquita Chamblee, "Knowing How and When to Use Our Privilege as a Tool to Become Better Allies," Address, National Conference on Race & Ethnicity from Southwest Center for Human Relations Studies, National Harbor, Maryland, June 1, 2010.

[17]   Ibid.

[18]   Kathryn Russell, "Checklist for White Allies Against Racism," Cortland Edu., 2001, http://web.cortland.edu/russellk/courses/hdouts/raible.htm.

[19]   Lee Gardenswartz and Anita Rowe, *Diverse Teams at Work: Capitalizing on the Power of Diversity* (SHRM, 2001).

[20]   Paul Kivel, *Uprooting Racism: How White People Can Work for Racial Justice* (New Society Publishers, 2011).

[21]   Stephen M.R. Covey, *The SPEED of Trust: The One Thing That Changes Everything* (New York: Free Press, 2008).

[22]   St. Francis Assisi, "Make Peace Prayer of St. Francis of Assisi," Catholic News Agency, http://www.catholicnewsagency.com/resources/saints/saints/peace-prayer-of-st-francis-of-assisi/.

[23]   Stephen M.R. Covey, *The SPEED of Trust: The One Thing That Changes Everything* (New York: Free Press, 2008).

[24]   Ibid.

[25]   Ibid.